On

a

Dark

Night

I

Left

My

Silent

House

On a Dark Night I Left My Silent House

PETER HANDKE

Translated from the German

by Krishna Winston

FARRAR STRAUS GIROUX

New York

Farrar, Straus and Giroux

19 Union Square West, New York 10003

Copyright © 1997 by Suhrkamp Verlag Frankfurt am Main

Translation copyright © 2000 by Farrar, Straus and Giroux, LLC

All rights reserved

Distributed in Canada by Douglas & McIntyre Ltd.

Printed in the United States of America

Designed by Abby Kagan

First published in 1997 by Suhrkamp Verlag, Germany, as In einer dunklen Nacht ging
ich aus meinem stillen Haus

First published in the United States by Farrar, Straus and Giroux

First edition, 2000

Library of Congress Cataloging-in-Publication Data
Handke, Peter.
    [In einer dunklen Nacht ging ich aus meinem stillen Haus. English]
    *On a dark night I left my silent house / by Peter Handke ; translated from the
German by Krishna Winston.*
        p.   cm.
    ISBN 0-374-17547-0 (alk. paper)
    I. Winston, Krishna. II. Title.
PT2668.A5 I4813 2000
833'.914—dc21   *00-039318*

Although this story does have something to do with the village of Taxham near Salzburg, it has little or nothing to do with any pharmacist or other living persons there.

On

a

Dark

Night

I

Left

My

Silent

House

At the time when this story takes place, Taxham was almost forgotten. Most residents of nearby Salzburg couldn't have told you where it was located. To many of them, even the name sounded foreign. Taxham? Birmingham? Nottingham? And in fact the first football club after the war was called "Taxham Forest," until it climbed out of the lowest category and received a new name, then, over the years, worked its way up in the standings and even became "FC Salzburg" (by now it may have backslid to an earlier original name). Although in the center of town people often saw buses with TAXHAM on their destination sign drive by, neither more full nor more empty than the rest of the buses, hardly a single townsperson had ever sat in one of them.

Unlike the old villages in Salzburg's orbit, Taxham, founded after the war, never became a tourist attraction. There was no cozy inn, nothing to see—not even anything off-putting. Despite having Klessheim Castle, the gambling casino, and the official reception mansion just beyond the meadows, Taxham—neither a section of town, nor a suburb, nor farmland—had been spared all visitors, from nearby or from any distant parts whatsoever—in contrast to all the other villages in the region.

No one came by, even briefly, let alone spent the night. For there was never a hotel in Taxham—again in contrast to Salzburg, both the town and the province—and its "tourist rooms" consisted of niches, refuges, hideaways of last resort, available when everywhere else the signs read "no vacancy." Not even TAXHAM, the name that formed a ghostly trail of light on the front of the buses circling until late at night through the now darker, more silent center of Salzburg, seemed ever to have lured anyone out there. No matter whom you asked, including the most open-minded and especially the most broad-minded, said, when questioned about Taxham, "No," or merely shrugged.

Perhaps the only strangers who went there more than once were my friend Andreas Loser, teacher of classical languages and self-nominated liminologist, and I. The first time I visited Taxham, I found myself on the main thoroughfare, called

"Klessheim Avenue" (no trace of castle or avenue), and stopped in a little shack of a bar, where a man railed for hours about how he'd been itching to kill someone: "No help for it!" And it was Andreas Loser who, one winter evening in the almost empty restaurant at the Salzburg airport (in those days almost larger than the arrival hall), whispered to me, "Look, that's the pharmacist of Taxham sitting over there!"

Since then my friend Loser has gone who knows where. And I left Salzburg long ago. And at the time when this story takes place, the pharmacist of Taxham, with whom we got together quite often after that, hadn't been heard from in almost as long—whether that was like him or not.

That Taxham seemed so inaccessible stemmed from its location, and the settlement itself was also responsible.

Something that's happening to all sorts of places these days was characteristic of Taxham from the beginning, namely being cut off or at least made hard to get to from the surrounding area and neighboring towns by all sorts of transportation lines—especially long-distance ones—impossible to cross on foot or by bicycle. In contrast to towns now, which get squeezed only little by little into such a spandrel world, isolated and hemmed in by the expressways proliferating on all sides, Taxham had come into being with such barriers already in place. Although it lay in a broad river valley and on the threshold of a city, it rather resembled a military camp, and in fact, its immediate vicinity, with the German border very near, actually had three military bases, one of them within the township itself. The rail line leading to Munich and beyond, one of Taxham's barriers, had been there far longer than the village, and the highway, too, had been built even before the Second World War, as the Reich autobahn (decades later the Reich eagle, carved, along with the date of construction, at the entrance to the tunnel-like underpass, still had the swastika clutched in its talons), and similarly the airport, built during the first Austrian republic, made it hard to reach the site of the future village.

Built into this transportation-corridor triangle, reachable almost only by circuitous, inconvenient routes and through underpasses, Taxham appeared as an enclave, and not only at first sight.

An enclave of what? Belonging to what? It was primarily, and certainly more conspicuously than anywhere else around Salzburg, a colony of war refugees, expellees, emigrants. In any case, the pharmacist was such a person, a member of a family that had run a pharmaceuticals factory in the east, first under the Hapsburg monarchy, then in the Czechoslovak Republic, then under German occupation. More details, I said, I didn't want to know for this story of his, to which he responded, "That's fine! Leave it vague!"

And after the war, new arrivals like this hadn't merely settled in the spandrel between the long-distance train tracks, the highway, and the airfield, on what was left of farmland there, specifically the farm known as "Taxham"—long since gone—but had screened themselves off even more, barricaded themselves in.

After getting past the external obstacles, you came upon a sort of second encircling barrier, not preexisting but created intentionally. Whether beyond the railroad embankment or beyond the runway fence: Taxham appeared to be surrounded a second time, in its inner sphere, by embankments, and above all fenced in, if not with wire then with dense hardwood hedges as tall as trees, so tall that almost the only thing that showed above them was the tower of the one Catholic church, a postwar structure of worked stone (the Protestant church remained invisible from a distance).

The strips of land between the two systems of barriers, the externally imposed one and the internally added one, served as a football field, a park, or a scruffy open area, where you could see the pale ring left by the circus that came to town for a few days every year; altogether, these stretches had something like a bulwark about them.

And in another respect, too, Taxham was a forerunner by half a century, though on a much smaller scale, of many of the new housing developments known today as "new towns": hard to find your way in, and even harder, whether on foot or by car, to get out again. Almost all the routes that promise to lead you out then turn off and take you around the block or wend their way back past cottage gardens to your starting point. Or they simply dead-end at yet another impenetrable hedge, through which open land and whatever leads elsewhere can just barely be glimpsed, even if the street is named after Magellan or Porsche.

In fact, because of the adjacent airport, most of the streets (or rather access roads) of this bushy-hedged village of Taxham bear the names of pioneers of flight, like "Count Zeppelin," "Otto von Lilienthal," "Marcel Rebard"—presumably foisted on the immigrants after the war, without consultation; they themselves would probably have preferred "Gottscheer Strasse" or "Siebenbürger Strasse," but who knows? The only aeronautical street name that would have been really suitable, according to my friend Andreas Loser, was "Nungesser and Coli," after the two pilots who attempted the first trans-Atlantic flight and vanished soon after leaving the continent behind.

And in a third respect, too, from its beginning Taxham anticipated a contemporary phenomenon, so to speak: Just as today it's more and more common for people not to live where they work, it was already the rule fifty years ago for those with jobs in the spandrel- and hedge-colony to have their house or apartment somewhere else—not far from Taxham, but at least not in the village. The retailers and restaurant owners came only during the day, to run their businesses. Even one of the priests assigned to the settlement, a man I knew well, came there only to celebrate Mass, and actually lived in Salzburg, where he wandered around aimlessly (I've heard meanwhile that he gave up his post long ago).

The pharmacist also had his house outside of Taxham, near one of the farm villages close to the border-marking Saalach

River, just before it flows into the Salzach, in the natural spandrel or "point" there.

Yet he was fond of the place where he worked. His life unfolded in the triangle between his house by the river embankment, the pharmacy, and the airport, where in the period when we first met—his story takes place during another time altogether—he regularly ate his evening meal, sometimes with his wife, sometimes with his mistress.

The pharmacy, founded by his much older brother, had been the first business after the war in the new or temporary settlement of Taxham, indeed the first public institution open to all—before the school, the two churches, even before any shops. Not even a bakery preceded it (initially bread could be purchased at the original farm). For quite a while the pharmacy was the only place providing "services to the public," the postwar new arrivals. According to my acquaintance, people at first made disparaging jokes about this medicine hut in the no-man's-land, but gradually it became the provisional community center.

Even decades later you could still feel some of this: Although by now every trace of agriculture had disappeared and the pharmacy no longer stood alone but was flanked by church towers and supermarkets, it still let you imagine—more than see—a center of town.

Yet this impression certainly didn't come from the building itself. From the outside it looked like a tobacco shop or newsstand. And inside it had neither the dark, cleverly laid out, almost museum-like elegance of many older pharmacies nor the light, bright variety—where am I? in a solarium? a perfumery? a beach stall?—of so many new or recent pharmacies. It was almost alarmingly devoid of color or decoration, with not a single item, whether medicine or toothpaste, specially displayed, and the entire stock kept at a distance behind rather massive and ungainly barriers and glass-fronted cabinets, as if the items weren't wares for sale but an arsenal off limits to the unauthorized, monitored by two or three white-clad guards. It didn't even have that special threshold at the entrance, which, according to Andreas Loser, was so characteristic of pharmacies almost the world over—here you had no sense of elevation, no stumbling block, but instead drawings, ornaments, and patterns, richer than at the entrances to houses and quite a few other pharmacies, and a hollow even deeper than in church doorways; you found yourself inside the medicine warehouse just like that, without crossing a threshold.

"The Eagle"—that was the name of Taxham's pharmacy, chosen by the founding brother, who'd long since moved west, to Murnau in Bavaria, and established himself, along with his daughters, sons, and grandchildren, in the "Red Boar Pharmacy." But given its appearance, somewhere between a newsstand and an electric-company utility building, a more appropriate name would have been "the Hare" or "the Hedgehog," as the current owner acknowledged, or, if he'd had his druthers, it would have been called "Tatra Pharmacy," after the land of his fathers.

No, what set the flat structure apart from the others, which even for Taxham were far more prepossessing, was its location there at the center of the village, now almost as built up as a town: surrounded by an expanse of lawn disproportionately large for the masonry hut—almost a meadow, sparsely dotted with trees, old but not very tall, and shrubbery ditto, like relics of a former steppe. "Sometimes in the morning, when I'm going to work, I see smoke rising from the cottage there," says the pharmacist in his not purely Austrian way of expressing himself.

He was also fond of the trip back and forth, between his house by the river and his hedged-in shop, and of the evening trip from there along the runway fence to the airport, and so on (until one day there was no more and-so-on). He either walked to work or drove one of his big cars—always the latest model—but also occasionally rode a bicycle, black and heavy, a "Flying Dutchman," his back very straight, and a couple of times I saw him riding a motorbike along the country lanes; he was splattered with mud yet strangely reflective, as if returning from a fierce hunt (and once, in a dream, he landed in front of the pharmacy in his private blimp, shimmying down a rope into the steppe grass).

Of course, the people of Taxham stopped in to see him before going to the doctor's, perhaps also hoping to spare themselves a visit. What's less well known is that as a rule they would ask for advice and help afterward as well. "More and more the doctors have become specialists. And sometimes I think I can see the big picture that they miss nowadays. And besides, with me the patients needn't fear a referral or an operation. And sometimes I can even really help them."

. . .

That could happen and did happen above all when he crossed off medications, instead of adding or substituting others—not all the prescriptions on the doctor's list, but one here and there. "My task is primarily selecting and eliminating. Making room, not on the shelves but in people's bodies. Making room and channeling currents. And of course, gentlemen, if you insist, I have everything in stock." At night the shop—barred, locked, barricaded—seemed like a bunker ("which you'd have to dynamite to get into").

And in fact there were quite a few people in the village whom he was able to help this way—"also because they let themselves be helped this way." And since his reputation didn't extend beyond the village—"Heaven forbid!"—it was clear at the same time that the pharmacist of Taxham was by no means a miracle healer.

The local residents were hardly out the door when they promptly forgot their gratitude, and therefore him as well. Unlike family doctors, businessmen, or football players, he wasn't a recognized figure on the streets and in the few pubs. No one talked about him, recommended him to others, sang his praises, or made fun of the pharmacist the way they do in the classic comedies. People who ran into him outdoors, outside his realm of competence, either ignored him—quite unintentionally—or failed to recognize him, even if just a few minutes earlier they'd gratefully shaken his hand across the "counter" inside.

Part of the reason was that whenever possible the pharmacist didn't go out in his white lab coat but rather in hat and suit, with a pocket square, and looked right past the pedestrians, of whom there weren't many in Taxham, keeping his eyes fixed on treetops, crops, and raindrops in the dust, and therefore, according to the childhood superstition, remaining invisible. And it must also be said that he, too, as soon as he left his bunker in the evening, never recognized any of the people outside as his customers, clientele, or patients—at most as Herr or Frau So-and-so. Unlike a doctor, who remained "the doctor" when he left his practice, the Taxham pharmacist ceased to be a pharmacist as soon as he locked up his shop.

Who or what was he then? One time I saw children running toward him. And although children usually run faster as they approach strangers, these children slowed down as they came near him and looked up at him, away from him, up at him.

At the time when this story takes place, it was summer. The meadows around the airport and around the hedged-in settlement beyond had already been hayed once, and by now the grass was high again, easy to mistake from a distance for the grain that was hardly grown in the region anymore; unlike the spring grass, it had almost no flowers, and depending on the wind, its green showed streaks of gray, or the other way around.

It was also the time of year with almost no fruit, the cherries having been harvested already or plundered by the birds, especially the ravens, and the apples being far from ripe, except for the nearly white-skinned early apples, though such trees were rarer than ever.

In Salzburg, to the east, the festival was already under way, but although even the most distant Alpine valleys, beyond the passes, tunnels, gorges, even borders, felt its reverberations, Taxham, right nearby, remained untouched, and only half of the advertising column out on the edge of the meadow and hedge had posters on it, like the rest of the year; the rounded surface toward the runway and the control tower was bare, as usual.

The local soothsayer—you always seem to find one in such places—had predicted at the beginning of the year that the region to the south of Taxham would experience a summer earthquake, and in fact this had just occurred, near Kapstadt. And according to the soothsayer, before summer's end a war would break out to the west of T., a three-day war, but with never-ending consequences!

He got up early, as usual, "with the first raven cries." His wife was still asleep, in the other part of the house. They lived together, yet had been separated for more than a decade, each in his or her own realm; they always knocked before entering, and even in the shared spaces—vestibule, cellar, garden—there were invisible and visible partitions, and where that wasn't possible, as in the kitchen, they occupied the space in shifts, as indeed they had experienced all of everyday life in shifted time ever since they'd broken up and in a sense gone their separate ways, so although it would have been natural earlier on for his wife to get up at the same time as he did, perhaps now she had to force herself to stay in bed? And force herself to stay in the house when he went out to the garden? And to go out to the garden when he stayed in the house? And to go away tomorrow on the solitary holiday she'd planned for herself, because he wanted to have the house and garden to himself all summer, as had been the case every year for a long time now?

"No," the pharmacist said. "We don't have any problems with each other. Only now is our life perfectly peaceful. The arrangement developed spontaneously, and we don't even notice it, or at most as a kind of harmony we never enjoyed before, which allows us to share things for a few minutes, in passing, to have something in common."

"Yes, in passing," his wife said. "In the wink of an eye. On the doorstep. Between window and lawn chair. Between tree-top and cellar window."

"What, for instance?" I asked.

The answer, once from her, once from him: "Always in silence. — When we're both listening to what the neighbors are saying. — Or to people walking along the dike on the other side of the fence. — Especially when a child's crying somewhere. — When an ambulance siren wails. — When we're in our own rooms at night and see through the window the emergency flare flashing up in the mountains over on the other side of the border. — When in last spring's flooding the drowned cow floated down the river. — At the first snowfall. — Yes? Oh, well. I don't know."

.   .   .

The sun rose. Not a drop of dew in the garden after the warm, dry night. But a sparkle from the apple tree: a hardened lump of sap exuded by a twig there, with a first ray of light shining through it now, a tiny lamp. The swallows high in the air deep black, as if it were still dawn. Only when one of them briefly raised its wings straight up as it swooped was there a flash of light up there, too, the sun gleaming on its feathers; it was as if the bird were playing with the morning light.

He butted his head against one of the already fat apples hanging at eye level, as if it were a ball, but more gently; then he walked upstream on the dike and let the morning and mountain-water air buffet him. No one else was out and about, and, as they always did in summertime, the rock-strewn banks of the Saalach took up more space than the actual shore and water flow; they stretched, bright and bleak, seemingly all the way to the river's source in the distant lime-stone mountains.

The pharmacist thought of his dead. His son also came to mind. But he wasn't really dead, was he? No, he'd thrown him out. Or was that too strong an expression? Hadn't he simply given him up, lost sight of him, put him out of mind, forgotten him? "No, I threw him out," he said. "I threw my child out."

He swam in the river, which chilled him to the bone, first fighting the powerful current, then letting himself drift, almost exactly along the line in the river where the German border ran. The bushes along the banks rushed by incredibly fast, in a gallop. He dove so deep into the water that little pebbles being washed along the river bottom got swept into his ears, where for quite a while they jostled each other, scraping and rattling. He felt as if he could stay under water this way forever, without breathing, and as if from now on this would be his life.

Then the pharmacist almost forced himself to head for the bank, just before the steep drop-off farther down. An early plane was coming in for a landing, already low over the treetops, and in one of the windows he made out a child's face. That was how keen his eyesight was, and not only after his swim in the icy river. And maybe in that respect the name his brother had given the pharmacy in Taxham was justified.

At home he showered, rinsing off the gray, chalky river water, and drank the coffee that had been brewing during his swim, Blue Mountain Coffee from Jamaica, the best coffee he could get in this area, as always. Not a sound from his wife's part of the house, while her suitcase was already standing down in the vestibule, with an airplane ticket resting on top, which he hadn't looked at. "Just as before each of her departures, I suddenly found myself picturing the strawberry slope," he said, "the spot she once told me meant summer to her when she was a child."

He'd traveled a great deal himself when he was younger, almost all over the world. By now nothing tempted him anymore, not a single place. Right here, in this very location, he felt every morning as if he were setting out, or had set out long ago, and today would put the next stage of the journey behind him. "I wanted to stay here, much longer, much longer."

Now on the dike, visible through the garden shrubbery only by the bright colors of their outfits, the first runners, in pairs, single file on the narrow path (but in Taxham, beyond the meadows, almost no one ran, even to catch the bus), talking too loudly, as if they thought their voices wouldn't carry otherwise.

And from one of the neighboring properties a child's shriek and then crying—heartrending—and then promptly the same from the house on the other side. He listened. And he was sure that his wife was also listening behind her door. They listened together, even when the crying and sobbing to left and right had died down and had long since given way to talking and calls back and forth, with voices that seemed clearer and more resonant after the earlier bawling. They also heard the train go by over on the German side. "Heading for Bad Reichenhall."—"Yes."

On this particular morning the pharmacist rode his wife's bicycle; she wouldn't be needing it for the next few weeks in any case. He took the road parallel to the river bank, then a stretch through the meadows along the river, then turned off and rode through the fields to the farm village of Siezenheim. The cemetery there had a piece of conglomerate with a crucified Christ—without the cross—scratched into the rock, the cross indicated only by Christ's posture—a hydrocephalic head on a Lilliputian body, the little arms spread wide, the grooves in the east-facing rock, usually hard to make out, weathered almost beyond recognition, appearing deeper and more distinct in the morning light.

And then the pharmacist chose to continue in an easterly direction, riding into the sun: In that way he avoided having his shadow in front of him, a sight he'd always found upsetting. From the grass, as earlier from the river and then from the grooves in the stone, rose the smell of the last few weeks' drought (the stories you heard about Salzburg and all its rain were often wrong). As he reached the camouflage-spot-colored barracks of the Siezenheim army base, a city bus drove by, painted and decorated for the festival as if it, too, were part of these camouflage-colored façades; an airplane's shadow swooped over the ground like the blink of an eyelid.

As he turned off into the hedged-in settlement, or, as he secretly called it, the "Lost Island," someone said hello to him—a rarity here—then a few others, between Lindbergh Promenade and Lilienthal Avenue, the greeting followed each time by embarrassment—until finally the pharmacist realized that the greetings were directed toward the familiar clunky prewar bicycle, usually associated with his wife, the "lady pharmacist" (which, in fact, she was, as almost everyone in the family was a pharmacist, in both the older and the younger generations, with the exception of his son).

His two employees, an older woman and a young man, still almost a child—the woman was his mother, for here, too, pharmacy work was a family tradition—were already waiting on the grassy plot at the center of the village, lounging, overpunctual as always, outside the barred entrance to the bunker, with a good-weather cloud high overhead. They'd come from the south years ago, fleeing the civil war, and had brought with them a curse commonly hurled at enemies there: "May your only inn become the pharmacy!"

The pharmacist also had a daughter, who'd been working with him lately, since completing her studies, but for the summer she'd left the Lost Island for another, together with her boyfriend, he, too, a pharmacist, but also—a novelty in the family!—a physicist.

At her departure he'd had the impression that she was reluctant to go and for the first time, curiously, was worried about him. Yet it seemed—as it always had, incidentally—that precisely her absence, or the absence of all those close to him, protected him, or so he thought at least, just as this absence also compelled him to do everything, or to live in such a way, that the other person could stay away for as long as originally intended, and calmly, free of worry, fully savoring the trip, the island paradise, and—why not?—happiness.

The absences of his family members—"a pharmacist doesn't have friends, or at least I can't picture having any," he said—also gave him an existential jolt every time. "If I could formulate a moral or lifelong imperative for myself," he said, "it would be this: Comport yourself in such a way that the relatives who happen to be absent at any given moment—relatives in the broadest sense—can always stay far away without you, in a good state of mind, unperturbed!"

"And if none of the relatives is away?"

"One of them is always away."

Like quite a few pharmacy employees perhaps, the two in Taxham were something more than just clerks; in fact, they were salaried employees. Or at least, with the passage of time they had come to be viewed as more than clerks by the customers, or rather advice-seekers. And as a result, the refugee woman and her son no longer had anything subservient about them, but were considered authorities and acted accordingly. Their work gave them more satisfaction than that of ordinary salespeople, presumably.

For that reason the pharmacist let them work as much as possible on their own, and not only since this particular summer—and of course it helped that there were far fewer hypochondriacs or sufferers from anxiety or despair: as if others, not only he, benefited from the summer absence of family members; it cheered them up, gave them strength, a very special medicine.

And that allowed the pharmacist to retreat into the back of the shop for as much as half the day. "I can't be around people all day," he told me. "And why should I, anyway?" For the most part, the preparing of medications in pharmacies had become pretty much superfluous. But he still enjoyed working with a few basic ingredients now and then, transforming them into another substance by means of techniques learned long ago, or simply being there, after mixing them, to see them transform themselves through spontaneous reactions. Such production—physical as well as chemical—of headache remedies, heart drops, arthritis salves, was expensive, time-consuming, and for the moment seemingly pointless, since out in front the same things were available, in the same form, with hardly different tastes or smells, and, furthermore, factory tested.

Yet he couldn't break the habit of doing things from scratch. In his imagination he was keeping in practice for hard times that weren't far off, hard times that would affect not so much him as the others, his customers, the people from the village, the immediate environs (actually this was all there was, for no one came from the outside, except during his infrequent night duty). And his hand motions were nothing like what people, or people like us, probably associate with a "pharmacist"; they weren't painstakingly precise, carried out in a confined space, "picky," but rather expansive, with running starts, retreating, swooping down, beating the air.

Once, during an attempted robbery—the first, by the way, since the pharmacy's founding—the intruder came upon the pharmacist thus occupied in the back room, and promptly dropped his knife and fled: "But he also noticed that I wasn't afraid. At moments like that you musn't be afraid."

"How do you manage that?"

"You musn't be afraid."

The pharmacist even had a specialty. He was an expert—to the extent it's even possible with such an infinitely varied subject—on mushrooms.

Many pharmacies, at least European ones, post charts in the window at the beginning of summer, with pictures of the edible and especially the poisonous varieties, sometimes even set up three-dimensional models, carefully arranged in real moss. But when an inexperienced gatherer comes in from the woods and fields with the real mushroom he's found and asks for information, most pharmacists just shake their heads without a word, or perhaps tap the earthy things lightly from a distance—please, no sand on the glass counter—and almost invariably issue unfavorable oracular judgments: poisonous, or at least highly suspicious.

But the Taxham pharmacist knew at a glance, or at first touch, or at the latest from sniffing or nibbling, what people had brought him (he could identify several almost indistinguishable varieties by the different worms, snails, earwigs, or spiders on or inside them). And above all, he showed enthusiasm for every mushroom placed before him, even when just a few gills of one, stuck to a child's hand and then thoughtlessly popped in the mouth, could do very bad things, even when the mushroom in question stank and oozed in all directions like a three-week-old carcass.

"I often wonder whether it wasn't my passion for mushrooms that drove my wife and me apart," he said. "Especially in the fall, when I came home in the evening, all my coat and suit pockets would be stuffed with them, and then the refrigerator, too, and the pantry, and even the cellar, where mushrooms keep best, with their aroma. Day after day she had to eat my mushrooms—there are far more edible kinds than people think—and well into the winter. Of course, after a while I stopped bringing them into the house, but then I hid them from her in the garden—how could I throw away mushrooms, these splendid gifts of nature?—and out there they glowed and gave off their unmistakable smell from under the shrubs and from holes in trees, the worst smell of all, like a dog's cadaver, being that of the stinking morel, which, when it's young, no bigger than a pigeon's egg, is a delicacy not described anywhere as yet, for instance cut up raw and served with salt and olive oil."

Thus the second thing the pharmacist pursued in his laboratory, or rather his kitchen, was his mushroom studies, where he was sometimes the self-assured chef, sometimes the diffident apprentice, slow on the uptake; yes, he was even preparing a very special mushroom guide, in which he planned first to highlight the virtues of some generally despised varieties and then explore the effect of certain mushrooms on the eater—but he wasn't concerned with the psychoactive species, the so-called consciousness-expanding ones, so much as with the "dream mushrooms," the "dreamexpanding" ones.

Yet at the beginning of the time when his story takes place, the area around Taxham, and not that area alone, was suffering from a major drought. There were no mushrooms far and wide, and since the pharmacist needed actual samples for his project, especially for describing their smell, on this particular morning he didn't get far with his mushroom fantasies; at most he could cross out observations in his notes that he intended to omit or skip.

From the counter running the length of the wall with the large plate-glass window, he could see the parched lawn in back of the building, onto which a blackbird trotted again and again—only blackbirds could pop so unexpectedly into nowhere—with a black, shiny, seemingly eyeless head, a knight in search of single combat, his visor already closed. The hedge from which the bird always burst forth formed the beginning of a series of staggered hedges extending all the way to the high hedge on the horizon marking the end of the village, where, as the pharmacist could clearly see, only one leaf was stirring, but that all afternoon, a furious flickering and fluttering, standing for an entire tree and, in time, for an entire forest.

In between he could be found in the front room helping out, even if only bringing a glass of water.

At noon the pharmacist went out for a snack, as was his habit, to the wooded area between Taxham and the Salzburg airport. Habit? It was more a matter of certain rituals or self-imposed rules that he observed strenuously, even though he sometimes had to force himself.

A stranger coming through these woods would have perceived them as shady, in every sense of the word. Even for the local residents, they weren't a destination. At most they drove by fenced portions on a road that was oddly winding for this plain. The fencing was unusual for woods anywhere in this country, and was interrupted by short wood roads that apparently soon came to a dead end in the underbrush. They had deep tire tracks, and were littered with trash, seemingly not only from vehicles on the ground but also from the hundreds of small aircraft passing overhead every day; even the trees had scraps of paper and plastic caught in them, all the way up to their crowns.

But the pharmacist knew a second forest within this forest. This copse was surrounded by a ditch and a girdle of brambles, with a breach in one spot where he could enter by way of a plank, without even having to duck. After the semidarkness outside, it was light in here, as if in a clearing, yet many things were growing here, providing shade, but each tree or bush clearly at a distance from the next, off by itself—and thus the shadows were also separate—and as a rule only one of each variety—one raspberry bush, one birch, one pine, and so on, in a circle, but all random, without order, which precluded the impression of being in a tree or plant nursery. Also there were things growing here that were very unusual for the area and wouldn't have been considered possible, such as a Spanish chestnut, a Serbian spruce (a survival from the Ice Age, thin as a rod but towering above the others), a mulberry tree, a sycamore.

When he sat down with his old, cracked briefcase under the beech—it, too, a unique exemplar—the tree with the broadest shade there, he saw that he wasn't alone for a change. A few shadows over, a group of woodsmen lay stretched out on the ground, taking their midday break, with their tools—saws and ladders—next to them. They'd set fire to a big pile of roots they'd dug out, and the fire was burning brightly, without smoke, another unique feature among the others. The pharmacist ate like them: the sandwiches he'd brought along in his briefcase—theirs were very similar—and, for dessert, an apple (from the Taxham supermarket).

"Pharmacist?" The smell of medicine, which, whether he wanted it or not, clung to him in his workplace and for a while after he left it—at any rate his car was always filled with it, and he sometimes avoided the car for that very reason—had dissipated long since, on the way. And his clothing was so inconspicuous that in cut and color, at least there and at this moment, it was hardly distinguishable from that of the woodsmen. And besides, he was barefoot like them, had already taken off his shoes coming in: Noon was the time of day when he felt a great weakness inside him, and not from hunger, so it helped him to have the ground directly underfoot, especially in these woods, where for a few steps the path was soft with recently fallen piles of chestnut blossom strings, but then for instance offered a stretch with nothing but the hard ridges of protruding roots, and finally ended here in a veritable field of angular, sharp beechnuts, a massage from his feet to the ends of his hair.

They all ate their midday meal in complete silence, and remained silent for a good while afterward. If they looked in the same direction, each did so independently of the others. The man from the beech drank from the clearing's hidden spring under the sycamore in such a way that the others could watch him, then went back to his place, while the workmen had already resumed their cutting and sawing, and read, as he usually did in summertime, one of the medieval epic tales of knights and magic.

"Weren't those epics actually meant for wintertime— telling of blossom freshness and bathing in the lake, while the castles were snowed in and isolated?"

"But in the summery landscapes they describe I can also recognize the current summer world, the world of today; it appears more distinctly before my eyes, and as something that by now has become a fact, no longer merely a magic and fairy-tale trick."

"For example?"

"See above, see below. Or you fight your way for hours through the underbrush, and suddenly a door opens automatically in front of you, and someone takes your bag from you in an air-conditioned hall and escorts you to the next adventure."

"A so-called adventure?"

"No, a real one. In that plantation, the forest-within-the-forest, one early afternoon, while I was reading, and especially in the intervals of closing my eyes, whole subterranean hosts were seated there, gray on gray, but poised for action, ready to show their true colors, and they were sitting in their saddles not over there, under the transparent mountain, the Untersberg, with Charlemagne, but here beneath the summery plain."

He still had to go into town for the monthly meeting with his colleagues, the "pharmacist of Taxham," whom his colleagues knew only as such, not by his name.

For him the meeting was not at all inconsistent with the hour he'd just shared with the woodsmen, who moved through the light and shadow cast by the single trees as if they were riding, whereupon he leaped into the saddle and rode toward them; it was odd, though, that such things happened to him only with these outsiders, or outcasts even. Because he was a refugee, or descended from refugees, and had always seen himself as outside the community, tied to no community (if also long since without regret)? Because he was always working in the outer districts, neither village nor town, without a town council and proper authorities?

No explanations, no reasons—"leave it vague." At any rate, at the meeting and for a longer time afterward the beechnut smell on his hands still awakened associations of a deck of cards.

Above the woodsmen's heads, clouds had drifted by and single-engine planes had droned. The pharmacist of Taxham had been overcome there by hunger, first an actual physical hunger, for fruit—but there was hardly any to be found, only a dried-up wild cherry and an equally dried-up currant, from a lone bush, an escapee from a garden—and then an undefined hunger, with no particular object, but a ravenous hunger, a drive? a compulsion?

Even the dead black mole he saw on the way back, its pointy face in profile, had reminded him again of a knight's visor. It was that transitional time of year when nature, otherwise his province, so to speak, had nothing to offer—no fruits, no mushrooms, nothing. Normally he missed having something to gather. But this time, he told himself, it freed him—for something else? "A good thing there was nothing to gather?"

In the center of Salzburg the pharmacist moved around as if wearing a cap of invisibility. During all those years I saw him face to face only twice. Although he told me he wasn't close to anyone in town, I did catch him there, though each time by means of a singular visual detour.

One time I was walking along a little-used path on the Mönchberg when I saw the Spanish prime minister coming toward me, casually dressed, accompanied by a broadshouldered man in dark clothing, wearing sunglasses—his bodyguard, no doubt—whom I recognized only after we had passed each other as the pharmacist of Taxham.

And likewise another time, as I was crossing the Staatsbrücke, I saw, on a balcony of the "Österreichischer Hof," an American movie actress famous at the time (she later drowned in the Pacific), who was giving a small, almost shy wave to someone below—certainly not me? No, for as I looked around, I saw an elegant foreigner—a rarity in this town— but dusty and ravaged like a second Richard Widmark, waving to her the same way—it couldn't be the pharmacist from the outskirts, could it?—yes, it was him, and gone already, as was the beauty from her hotel balcony.

The monthly meeting with the other members of his guild was summery and short: Several pharmacies were closed for the holidays, and most of the new drugs weren't scheduled for release until fall; for now, at least in this area, the old standbys were sufficient, though because of the tourists larger supplies had to be laid in; this didn't affect the Taxham pharmacist.

The three of them then lingered on a terrace above the Salzach, where a faint breeze off the river fanned the heat away—the pharmacist from Itzling, the pharmacist from

Liefering, and him. The pharmacist from Itzling was a young woman, to whom the Taxham pharmacist had once remarked, in the middle of another conversation about medications, quite absent-mindedly and unintentionally, "You're really very beautiful."

He told me later that there was also a story to tell about this woman, at least as adventurous and mysterious as his own, and certainly more erotic—she would make a good main character for a book. Why me, anyway? Why not her?—I responded by asking whether he could picture a heroine called "the woman pharmacist of Itzling." And altogether, he should just wait and see.

That afternoon, which I view as the beginning of his story, he again became lost in thought, with the two others there, and abruptly said to the beautiful pharmacist, "Why are you so brown? Among the ancient Egyptians only the men were brown; the women had to be white as alabaster or cheese. And why do almost all pharmacists nowadays go around with these permanent tans, and especially the women?"

"But you're tanned yourself, actually as dark as a *fellah*."

"That's my natural state, and it also comes from being out in the sun and shade and moving around, not like the rest of you from lying and applying lotion in the South-West Tanning Salon, where the rays are carefully calibrated to the white of your lab coats."

"Why are you being so mean today? There was a time when you wanted to erect a pyramid in my honor!"

All this time the ancient, almost deaf pharmacist from the outlying village of Liefering was expounding, in a voice that boomed across the river, his theory of the signs of the Zodiac, according to which these signs governed not only people but also regions and entire countries. The fate of nations depended on the stars that ruled them. The history of mankind, of the peoples' relationships with each other and individually, was determined by Leo, Scorpio, Gemini, or Taurus. Thus a United States of Europe was inconceivable simply because every European country had a different sign, all of them equally powerful; no country could claim an advantage. Even in Germany all the provinces had different constellations, incompatible with each other, for which reason the fear of this largest country, now acute again, was absolutely unfounded. On the other hand, one constellation ruled all of North America, and that was why the United States had come into being there, and of course stayed together, under the sign of Aries? Virgo? Capricorn?

"Nonsense!" the pharmacist of Taxham interrupted him suddenly, after looking back and forth between the young woman and the river for a while, lost in thought again. "Typical pharmacist's superstition! It doesn't come from up there, up in space, but from down here, from beneath the ground. And from down here we, or the countries and nations, if you will, aren't directed and constrained at all, but prodded, spurred on, set in motion."

"Where down here?" The young woman asked this, while the old man next to her went on spinning his stars-and-states theory at the top of his voice, without listening. "In the magma?"

But the man from Taxham had gone under again, had closed his eyes and even seemed to have stopped breathing. And he didn't move a muscle when the woman abruptly grabbed him by the chin and said, "Typical pharmacist's superstition!" The pharmacist from Liefering was just remarking, "That business in Yugoslavia had to end badly: above every country there, a star that was incompatible from the outset with the others and at war with its neighboring star."

He took the bus back to Taxham and worked there in the back room until after sundown—which was late in July—with the doors long since locked. Sometimes it seemed that time could be grasped in an image: now, for instance, in the image of a curve, in which he felt comfortably cradled as he worked silently away.

First the shop out in front was being cleaned, and then from one minute to the next a silence fell, in which, although the sun was already gone, colors predominated, then blossomed. Something had been pushed aside, an obstacle, a screen, a minimizing glass, and a different map of the world came into view, on another scale, not intended for entering, and certainly not for consuming or putting in your pocket, but perhaps for a certain kind of measurement-taking—even though, as the silence persisted, it had promptly faded and shriveled up. He spread his fingers and let the air blow between them.

He pushed himself away from the counter, several times. Through the open window, through the bars protecting the little building, came the smell of the settlement's dusty streets, just sprinkled, which gave him a whiff of the soaking rain they hadn't had in so long, and at the same time, swooshing in unexpectedly from beyond the last ring of hedge, a good Taxham mile away, the smell of the circus, although it had moved on way back at the beginning of summer.

If the pharmacist was known at all in the area—for instance by Andreas Loser and me—it was for his sense of smell. In Loser's case it was hearing and listening that counted, or, in his words, "moved his thoughts along," and in my case it was primarily seeing and contemplating; but with our distant acquaintance it was simply smelling—not any special sniffing, but just having something in his nose, without any special effort, hundreds of things at a time, without confusion, clearly distinguished. (And obviously the peculiarities of one couldn't always be separated from those of the other.) Just as some people could see a thing and keep its image on their retina for months afterward—they had only to close their eyes—time and again the pharmacist would have a smell from long ago in his nostrils, still fresh and even stronger than originally, a smell perhaps snapped up only in passing and long since subject to the statute of limitations, as it were. And just as those other people first perceived objects with real clarity and vividness in those residual images, so it was for the pharmacist with his residual smells.

So along with the wafted-away circus, a leopard or perhaps only a miniature ape promptly leaps out of the nearest bush. And the pharmacist, lost in thought again, climbed onto his lab counter, rolled up his sleeves, and teetered on tiptoe. Amazing the way shifting your perspective a bit from the familiar could sometimes shift the gaps, give things a different twist, rearrange the entire state of affairs. "Wasn't that also uncanny at times?"

"Nothing was ever uncanny to me," the pharmacist responded, long after the time when his story takes place: "At least not until that time."

From up there on the counter it could be seen that all the buildings in the settlement, forming, in that brightness without sunshine, a closed, wide-curving kraal, offered a perspective very different from the small pharmacy building at the kraal's center. Their orientation was completely at odds with the pharmacy's, even though it had been the first, the original structure in the village; they were set on an axis noticeably opposed to the pharmacy's, as if to show disdain for the little structure in the middle, or as if it didn't exist at all.

And then, in driving away, if you looked over your shoulder, the squat cube there on the remnant of steppe seemed to be turning its back on the surrounding area, not even belonging to the soil around it, a sort of random boulder. No child awake at this hour. Not a bird in the sky. Yet there was a cloud overhead, a large, grayish-white cumulus cloud, its upper edge crumpled in many places, drifting slowly eastward, as if on pilgrimage; as if it were pilgrimaging. It might also have been moving westward, and it might also have been morning.

The pharmacist had the habit of taking his evening meal at a restaurant, and still out toward the airport. Except that his new eating place was located outside all the concourses, constantly being added or expanded, also past the parking lots and even past a field of vegetables. The building had grown out of a root cellar, or been built onto it, and the small, low-ceilinged dining room was half underground, so to speak, as if from time immemorial. How nice to go down the few steps from the hardly traveled road, which still suggested the wagon road it had once been, especially nice now, with the light fading, when you could look back up the stairs and see nothing, nothing at all.

Unlike previously, the pharmacist now sat down alone to his evening meal, had already been alone for a long time, without a mistress, and his wife had joined him here only a few times in the beginning, until those fat-bellied mushrooms that turned blue as you sliced into them, then shaded into olive green, those mushrooms he'd collected and brought so the chef could prepare them, took on for her, when she was forced to eat them, "the taste of human flesh."

Outside, when he raised his head, dusk was falling over the fields, and the last plane was landing; there were no night flights.

The one other table that was usually occupied stood in the opposite corner, but because the place remained fairly quiet, in spite of the open door, the conversation there, between a couple and a man who turned out to be a priest in mufti, could be easily overheard, even though none of them were raising their voices. The couple's only child had run away and disappeared, years before. And in the course of the evening it came out that they had in fact thrown the child out, locked him out, then locked him out again, and finally put his satchel outside the door, no, a plastic bag, had rolled down the shutters and gone away on a trip, so as not to have to see what happened. And now their relationship was on the rocks, too. The woman: "I wish I were dead." The man: "Me, too."

The priest argued that dying was perhaps a kind of *salto mortale*, after which a person landed on his feet again, entirely different feet; but he got all muddled, began to stammer, fell silent; and then all three of them sat there in silence; the couple wept.

The Taxham pharmacist seemed invisible, and when he asked for the bill, he had to wave his arm several times. And when he said good-bye, he did so in a language that the proprietor took for Spanish. Spanish? He couldn't understand himself what he'd just said. It had been no language at all.

As he pedaled home across the river valley on his wife's bicycle, which was quite high, by the meadows, now pitch dark, he encountered a strong smell of sweat, which turned out, as he rounded the bend, to come from a squad of soldiers on a night march.

One of the families next door to him on the lane along the dike was still sitting out on the verandah, and he chatted with them for as long as it took him to open the garden gate (but the gate was unlocked, as was always the case when his wife left the house); over the others' hedge, their heads could hardly be made out. In one of his skylights—was that a light shining? no, the reflection of a street lamp far off. And something like a spiderweb attached itself to his face as he made his way to the door and also indoors in the vestibule, as if he'd been gone much longer than just for the day.

He switched the television on for a second, during which a man on the screen opened his mouth wide—and switched it off before he could say a word.

As usual when he had the run of the entire house and was no longer restricted to his own living quarters, he didn't know where to go; he had trouble finding his place. So long since he'd been in his wife's rooms—since the last time she went away for a while. And now he wandered back and forth there in the dim light—every other lightbulb was burned out—and then noticed that he was instinctively looking for a message or a sign intended for him. But there wasn't even a trace of their shared past, unless he counted, half hidden, a tiny picture of their son, taken in a photo booth and pasted into a panoramic landscape, barely visible in the crown of a tree, with his head pointing down, no less, like a rebus.

And how precariously she had positioned all her things, big and small, not only in her bathroom, but also in her part of the kitchen: The seemingly rigid order she'd left behind could be thrown into complete confusion if some little object were dislodged in passing. Either something was hanging by a single thread, or it was perched on a ledge, usually high up, or this group of crystal balls was poised, in what looked at first like a miracle, on a slanting surface—but not another step!— or, like this open salt dish, it would tip at the slightest push, despite the apparently level surface under it, because one of its feet was broken, or, like this bundle of pencils, would break without the slightest pressure, because the points were so sharp. And what if this happened to be the very sign he was looking for?

Back in his own part of the house, he turned his bed pillow over; nothing. Strange contrast between the two pillows: one quite creased, the other one, next to it, completely untouched and smooth, the ironing folds just as they had been for years, as if in a glass case, a bed in a castle, unoccupied yet comfortable, waiting for someone to return.

His daughter had phoned from the island where she was on holiday; she planned to stay a while longer; and then his wife, too: She had arrived safely, though she didn't say where.

He played a game of chess with himself, letting "the other person" win. Through the open casements the fast-flowing river could be heard, invisible behind the dike, along with the chirping of crickets, actually more a delicate, nonstop trilling from the dike, the underbrush, holes in the ground—that most summery of sounds. A veil shrouded the moon.

"What do you want?" one of the players said to the other. "Is there anything at all you still want?" "Yes, I want the continuation. I'm quite eager to see what happens next."

"With what? With whom?"

"With me. With us. With my story. With our story. But we're going to have to do our part. And by that I don't necessarily mean deep-sea diving or scaling the Himalayas."

"And how do you picture such a continuation, for instance?"

"Well, someone might jump in now through the open window and ask for help. Or hold a knife to my throat. Or tomorrow morning I might find a snakeskin next to me in the bed. No, it would have to be more than just a skin, and something more terrible than just a snake."

"And why does your voice sound so choked up?"

"My daughter just asked me the same thing, even my wife. My voice sounded as if it were coming from a deep well, one of them said, from down a manhole, said the other."

On this day the last thing the pharmacist did was practice throwing: the chess pieces into their box, which he moved a bit farther away for each toss.

Perhaps it was his dried mushrooms, of which he bit off some pieces, perhaps not: At any rate, that night he had two dreams that took place without him, beyond his person. In one of them, adjacent to the small cellar in his house were suites of underground rooms, one grand hall leading to the next, all sumptuously decorated, festively lit, yet all of them empty, as if in expectation, awaiting a splendid, perhaps also terrible event, and not just recently, but since time immemorial.

In the second dream, the hedge barriers to the neighboring properties were suddenly gone, removed by force or simply fallen away, and people could see into each other's gardens and onto each other's terraces, and not merely onto them, but also into every corner of their houses, now suddenly laid bare, and likewise one neighbor could see the other, which in the first moments caused immense mutual embarrassment and shame, but then gradually gave way to a kind of relief, almost pleasure. (It should also be noted that all these hedgeless houses appeared as pole or moor dwellings, each one with a boat tied up down below.)

But after that came, quite unexpectedly—was it still a dream? a blackness, and then there was nothing but this blackness, no action, no film, just the end of the film, the end, quite simply, of any kind of "I am," "you are," "he is," "they are," "you people are," a blackness that filled every inch of space so completely that it jolted the pharmacist out of his sleep; yet it didn't dissipate at that point; it remained.

"I'd actually forgotten," he said, "that a few days earlier I'd had a small black growth on my skin removed, and the lab results were due soon."

Had he slept all night on his back this way, with his legs crossed? Now and then, through the wide-open window, the seemingly tipped-over waning moon had appeared for just a moment, in a rapidly swelling wall of cloud, with its face pointing down.

TWO

Wind gusts, the smell of rain, fallen somewhere else. And now, in the first light of morning, it was that kind of dark, clear, wide-horizoned day that he loved and that he hoped would stay that way until evening. (The relentless summer sun and the blueness had been rather like eternal ice.)

On a dark day like this the smallest ordinary occurrences began to vibrate, like test starts for a departure. And at the same time peace and quiet all around, without any more mirages from the sun. A sense of transitoriness accompanying this dark clarity, also carefreeness: In harsh sunlight, the nocturnal blackness from before would have lingered much longer.

Out for a swim in the river behind the house. Without the sun, its water glistened in an entirely different way, and also seemed less icy. On the other side of the border, as he let himself float, a house appeared amidst the trees on the banks, a house that hadn't been there the day before? And yet was old?

Similarly, out in the garden, as he gazed at the pyramid of the distant mountain, he saw a rock wall emerge that had the shape and brightness of a sail—also new overnight? Involuntarily he stretched out his arms through this dark air, reaching for someone at hip level.

Reading his medieval epic. Curious that when the "loveliest meadow in the world" was evoked, you could be sure the hero would soon come upon some terrible sight—a bleeding knight on a stretcher, with his legs cut off and only half his head left, or a virgin hanged by her braids from a tree.

Was it raining already? No, tiny animals were dropping in a steady stream from the poplar in the garden—which explained the constant crackling in the grass and also on the pages of his book. And they couldn't be blown away: The harder the blowing, the more stubbornly they crouched among the letters on the page, moving on only when the wind died down. And a bat darted out of a bush, a leathery sound, a rarity in the morning hours? not on a morning like this, and you could also follow it with your eyes for a long time, as if it were flying more slowly than usual. The first birds in the sky not as high perhaps as in the usual blue, or higher after all? and at any rate at an altitude at which no airplane or even satellite would ever be seen.

The only thing that was loud: the ravens, the chief population, apparently, not only of this region, and long since changed from winter to year-round birds. For the most part they cawed out of sight, like old roosters that can produce only one note, but louder, and fairly high up in the air, and in between a powerful, low-pitched cackling, a blind pounding on a xylophone, as it were.

One among the thousands now showed itself, on the broad top of the cedar in the garden next door, it, too, noticed for the first time there this morning. The raven was gesticulating on the tip of one of the coati-shaped branches, displaying its profile, with a roundish fruit in its beak—the garden, and not only this one, was strewn with drops, fruits from somewhere else entirely, including pieces of mangos, lychees, kiwis—its feathers rumpled and in wild disorder, its wings snapped in many places, folded, extended, as if the bird had far more than one pair—or were several ravens perched there in a cluster? were they eating flies out of each other's feathers?

"Raven, come and speak!" And the raven came flying from the treetop, landed on the outdoor table by the open book and the Blue Mountain coffee, first executed a series of mute directional signals with its head and wings, and then said, ". . ."

When it took off, a fat maggot was writhing on the table where it had been standing. And there had been a stench from the bird's beak, and its head had had pale spots on it. "It's time to light the fuse!" it had said, among other things. And in fact over there, next to a rusty piece of a child's dart, something was poking out of the ground that looked like the white end of a fuse—which he lit, as he'd been ordered. "And cut your bread by hand, not with the machine." And it really seemed, when he did as he'd been ordered, as he if were cutting bread for others' breakfast as well.

Then, out in front of the house, the pharmacist washed his fairly new big car, almost as wide as the river-hugging lane on which he lived. He cleared out the back seat and felt ready, armed, and equipped, though with a vulnerable spot or two, which, on the other hand, again according to the raven, was "as it should be."

The windows open and, his hands on the wheel, another page read in the epic before he set out. No wind thus far on this dark day; instead, the breeze from the book. "From today till the end of the story no more newspapers!" (The raven.) And in fact the time when this story takes place wasn't news-paper time. Didn't someone shout his name just as he started up the car, from inside the house? from the riverbed behind it? piteously? for help? No, just the screeching of the raven again. "And from today till the end of the story you have no name anymore!" And a neighbor walked past the car without recog-nizing him inside.

His last glance at the moment of starting the engine was directed not toward the house but toward the mailbox out in front. At last: no longer that patch of sunlight, which, during the preceding summer weeks, had again and again created the mirage of a letter inside; this, too, an advantage of this dark, clear day—empty was empty.

Then, as he drove along, the sensation of a strength that didn't come from the vehicle at all, but instead was a strange, perhaps useless and ridiculous strength, one that might also be the symptom of a life-threatening illness? He was missing the raven, or whom? *"Urlage,"* that was a word in the medieval epic for war. "They rode off to the *Urlage.*"

On the evening of this day, after his work and research, almost invisible and almost without sound, in the hedge-settlement or on the Lost Island, the road to the root-cellar restaurant.

Only once in the course of the day had he exchanged a longish glance with someone, from his laboratory in the back, through the bars there, with a child who soared into view on a swing behind one of the hedges, amazingly high in the air for one so small; or had it been a dwarf?—at any rate, at the right time for such an exchange of glances, toward noon, as his strength dwindled.

The day had remained consistently dark and clear. And now, halfway between Taxham and the airport complex, by the Winding Forest—given this name because of the road that tediously followed its perimeter—it finally began to rain, for the first time this summer.

Off onto a wood road at once and out of the car. He sat down on a stump, with underbrush as a roof. A pebble tossed at a distant tree trunk: bull's-eye!

The pharmacy smell had already been gone for quite a while, or perhaps was still there, but in a different way—the first raindrops after weeks of drought. As yet just sporadic craters in the dust (yes, even the woods had a layer of dust a foot deep; you emerged with grayish-white powder all over your shoes), little clumps of earth rolling away under the impact of the drops, small pieces of bark flying away: Perhaps in just this way a new era had dawned once upon a time, or, after half an eternity of stasis and rigidity, something like time had first been set in motion.

Crouching down to see what was happening from close up; and besides, crouching you were closest to yourself. Yet the field of vision remained as broad as possible: the parked car, in which, with the increasing dusk all around, a curious brightness seemed to have been trapped, the seats very obviously empty, and as if there were more of them than usual, whole rows of them; beyond it the airfield with the last plane rising into the air, at one window that passenger who thought he could rub off the haze on the outside on the inside; to the right, on the highway, an almost endless convoy of trucks, white on white, United Nations troops deployed against a new war, or rather returning from there (a few trucks were also being towed, half burned out); to the left, the training place for police dogs, at the edge of the forest, where one of the dogs seemed to have just got caught in a culvert and was howling piteously, while another, growling almost as piercingly, kept leaping at a man hidden behind a wall, burying its teeth in the ball of cloth in which the "fleeing criminal" had wrapped his lower arm, then refusing to let go and hanging on stubbornly as the man ran in a circle with him, swinging the animal through the air.

The rain coming down harder, the field emptying out, perceptions growing dim, blurring, but in their place no greater clarity or memorable thoughts, for with them, too, a blurring almost to the point of cessation, nothingness: "Staring into the idiot box" was the name given to such a condition, actually more common among children.

And now it got dark faster than ever before, went completely black before his eyes, at one blow.

Or hadn't it been a real blow, powerful and from very close by, right on the spot on his forehead where a week before the small dark swelling had been removed? Or several blows, many, out of the pitch black?

And if he'd defended himself in this single combat, or nine-against-one combat, then only at the beginning, in full recognition that no defense, of whatever kind, would get him out of this predicament, but only putting up with it as long as possible.

And if anything became clear to him, at once, with darkness falling all around him and the blow striking his head, it was this: From now on, and for the foreseeable future, he couldn't take a single step without awareness of this new condition, which imposed itself on him as a sensation of being surrounded on all sides—though not so closely and seamlessly that there was no possibility of slipping through.

Had it been an ambush? "If it was an ambush," he told me much later, "then one staged by my ancestors—at least I smelled them on me a long time after the blow."

"Tell me more."

"No. You, the recording scribe, mustn't be the master of my story. After all, not even I myself am the master of my story. All I can say is this: When I'd gathered my thoughts, I was lying among the canes of the underbrush, as if I'd been hurled down there, scrunched up among the protruding roots, but not wet, even though it was pouring by now, as it can pour only around Salzburg. And I felt a curious joy inside me, or was it gratitude, or a kind of élan? Now things were as they should be. The struggle could begin. The blow in the dark had beaten the last of the pharmacy and laboratory smell out of me, and I would've been so happy just to stay there in the underbrush. I wanted to catch something, trap something, some wild animal. How quickly you could turn into a satyr, of a kind that never existed before. There in my bush basket a few drops of blood could be seen on the dry bed of leaves."

"Was it no longer pitch black?"

"No one should be the master of this story. So I'll mention just one more thing about that moment: A smell went along with the blow, a fragrance, or actually a sort of spice."

Before driving on, he aimed his car's extra-powerful head-lights into the hidden copse. Several trees he had visited earlier that day at noon were no longer there. The wild cherry, the sycamore, the Spanish chestnut, the beech poplar—yes, that remarkable hybrid had been there—were gone, or perhaps merely not visible in the torrential downpour, which hardly left room for any image.

Instead, inside the encircling thicket, a lot of human bodies, lying every which way, stuffed into bags that seemed to be tied at the top, with only a wet cowlick poking out here and there. Corpses? A battle? In fact, it was a company of soldiers, stretched out there into the underbrush, though probably only from exhaustion—from the night march of the previous day?—so exhausted that only one of them stuck an eye out of his sleeping bag in the glare of the headlights.

Then, to his amazement, except for the table reserved for him every evening, the root-cellar restaurant was full, even though only the chef's car was parked outside by the dirt road, in the turnout.

Were these passengers from a canceled flight, sent here from the airline counters beyond the vegetable field? But if so, they would probably all have been served the same thing, which wasn't the case. Yet they all seemed to know each other. At least they acted familiar with one another. Without conversations from table to table, glances went back and forth constantly, not those hasty, furtive glances often exchanged by strangers in restaurants, but attentive, wide-eyed, friendly, considerate ones, which at the same time left the fellow diners in peace. When he entered—ducking his head in the cellar's low doorway—no one turned to look. Yet an imperceptible jolt went through those present, a jolt of recognition, and as if they were happy that he was there, too. And he felt much the same: as if he'd already met these people somewhere—at any rate, it hadn't been anything unpleasant or bad, but had taken place under a favorable sign.

Nonetheless, even here he wasn't free for a second of his awareness of danger, the danger not merely of a collision but of complete destruction, the possibility, furthermore, that with a flick of the wrist, a slip of the hand, even a wrong breath, it could be too late.

He was shivering. He didn't want anyone to notice. Why not? After all, it could also come from being rain-drenched. And weren't some of the others shivering, too? They looked pretty well soaked, down to their shirts and blouses (from their light summer jackets, draped over the backs of their chairs, here and there little puddles dripped onto the old clay floor of the former root cellar, coated with a transparent sealer). Except that his particular shivering didn't come from some external factor but rather welled up from below, as if from the ground, and for moments at a time you couldn't tell whether it wasn't the earth that was shaking, violently, and not only at his feet. He had to grab hold of something, and in so doing dislodged the heavy table. The warmth from all those weeks of summer still lingered in the restaurant. No one could be cold.

"What is your desire?" (The proprietor's question; he knew him only as a guest, and otherwise neither his name nor his profession.) Even before the guest opened his mouth, he knew that not a single word would come out. He'd lost the power of speech, and for longer than just this moment. But then why had the blow and the blows back there in the pitch dark not been accompanied by any alarm, or by any fear of death? — For a long time now, he imagined, he hadn't been afraid of death anymore.

To lose the power of speech: What was that like? Like that sensation in dreams when you're supposed to run, flee, or, more likely, rescue someone, a close family member, the closest, from water, from fire, from the abyss, from a wild beast, from a Tasmanian devil, and you can't budge from the spot, as if you're weighted down with stones.

Nonetheless he now opened his mouth to speak, to express his desire, even passed his hand, as if casually, through the candle flame on the table, through the bluish transparency there, hoping that the pain would help get his dead tongue moving again. Not even a stutter. Not a sound.

And it wasn't that he had no desires. First of all, he was ravenous, as he hadn't been for a long time, probably also because of this rain, which made everything around, and not just the dishes on the menu, seem fresher and more appetizing.

And then, stimulated and dammed up by his loss of speech, another desire had awakened, or broken out, or broken through, tangible less inside him than simply in the air. There's the saying that a question is hovering in the room; with an entirely different justification, the same could be said here. Desire was hovering in the room. What kind of desire? A rather awkward, clumsy one, never acted upon or consummated, a desire that had pretty much gone out of use or possibly had never been in use, a childish, sheepish desire, ashamed of itself and thus inelegant, expressing itself badly and unclearly, easily mistaken for a toothache, stomachache, an urgent need to relieve oneself, or also for pleading for mercy.

He couldn't even manage to point on the menu to the food he so greatly desired. He merely gesticulated wildly. He knocked the proprietor's notepad out of his hand. Luckily the day's special was recommended to him, exactly

the one he wanted, and his head jerks were correctly inter-
preted as a nod.

"With all this rain, soon I'll be able to serve you your
mushrooms again, as a side dish," the proprietor said. And
then: "You have blood on your forehead, a lot of blood. An
accident? Did you hit the windshield?" And he personally
dipped a cloth in cold water and tied it around his head,
watched only by those at the very next table, without curiosity,
with silent sympathy, also with a kind of soothing attitude—
"It's not that bad!" and "The cloth looks good on you, could
have been made for you."

Then hours of nocturnal rain pounding on the roof of the
lodge. And this rain would continue for days in that area. It
was as if you could see all the people in the root cellar from the
rear, and from up high, without a roof, sopping wet and calmly
going on with their meal. Sometimes you saw yourself this
way in a dream, from the rear, with a couple of other total
strangers, as the heroes in an adventure movie, for which you
also made up the audience.

The guests left a few at a time, having paid cash, with large
notes that they peeled out of their pockets. They were picked
up either by taxis or by chauffeurs, who always dashed to the
door with umbrellas big enough for two. At least every other
guest bumped his head on the frame of the cellar door, and this
was true of one or two of the women as well, most of whom
were tall. As she went out, one of them said to him with a
quick smile, "Good luck!" And the others had an expression in
the corners of their eyes as they stood in the doorway—not an
actual movement, not a wink—that meant Good night! Yet all

of them had had something shabby and down-on-their-luck about them, and not only because of their unshaven faces, their stringy hair, their shambling gait: something profoundly broken and dilapidated, a help- and hopelessness, and as if none of them could even be sure of even making it through the night.

In the medieval book, open on his table, cleared in the meantime, a sword blow landed on someone whose heart then lay revealed in his chest.

He, too, paid right out of his pocket. (To be sure, this was nothing new for him.) The kitchen crew were already standing behind the glass partition, their arms at their sides or crossed, except for the dark-skinned dishwasher, who also seemed too big for the place, looking stooped not only over the faucet, but also while putting the dishes away on the shelves up above.

Another table was still occupied, as on the previous evening, this time by two men. Despite the dim light in the room, they were wearing sunglasses, and seemed even more down-at-heel than the other chance guests, or merely acted that way—how else could it be explained that the proprietor now brought them his guest book, which they both signed without hesitation?

And finally he recognized them. One was a winter sports champion once known far beyond the country's borders, a skier, who maybe three decades ago had brought home a gold medal from America, and that despite having lost one of his ski poles. And the man across from him was a poet who'd been famous in a different way, a refugee and foreigner, who was said in his day to have written a German that no native had in his head and which nevertheless made instant sense to many, especially the ordinary masses who heard him read his poems aloud.

And hadn't all the previous guests been celebrities of long standing, who had met here by chance, perhaps on the strength of an article praising the food and saying that here in the root cellar a famous person could "hide from the world"?

Whatever the case: the two remaining guests had sweat on their brows, and he smelled it at a distance as cold sweat, and also saw how every time the sweat had almost stopped, it would suddenly well up again. And intermittently the two would laugh again, at times with their whole faces, at times giggling, at times as heartily as only babies can laugh: Willy-nilly, and without knowing what it was all about, you had to laugh along with them. Were they giving him a little wave? Were they drunk? In the candlelight, rodents seemed to be dangling from their cheeks on both sides, their teeth sunk into the flesh.

Then he sat outside a while in his car without driving off immediately. Out here the nocturnal rain made an entirely different sound on the roof. Besides, he had a habit of simply sitting somewhere, gazing out the windshield or reading. In the days when he still traveled a lot, he'd often seen people sitting this way, alone in their cars by the sea, doing nothing, or reading, usually by steep cliffs, facing west, with or without a sunset, and he'd patterned himself on them.

How dark an airport could be, darker than any other civilized installations, and that included the runways, edged with ground lighting. The downpour had washed out a huge chunk of the tar applied to the former wagon road; it had slid down the bank, and poking out from underneath it were portions of a house used as fill, or even of a ship—a length of railing, a stairway down to steerage, an up-ended bow, out of which the sky-water was being sucked, with a loud gurgling sound, into hollow spaces lower down, into the belly of the house—or ship.

Now the two last guests were leaving the root-cellar restaurant, where the lights promptly went out behind them. Without coats or an umbrella, they were soaked the minute they stepped outside, yet they moved without haste, almost as if they were out strolling in this downpour, and had made up their minds to do this. He pulled up to them and motioned them to get in the car.

As they drove on, all three kept silent, until they were out of the spandrel between the take-off and landing runways, the highways and the railroad tracks, and also out of the natural spandrel or triangle of the confluent rivers. The man at the wheel kept silent because he was still struck dumb, and the two in back were sitting as if in a taxi, for whatever reason. They'd taken off their dark glasses. Their eyes were narrow and alert, and they didn't give off any smell now, or at most a whiff of wet hair, like scalded chicken feathers, at any rate nothing from their drenched clothes. When the heat blasting through the roomy car had dried these rather quickly, the former slalom champion slid into the seat next to him and began to address him.

That was during the drive through a tunnel, where the pounding on the car roof let up for a moment. The man had a curiously toneless, hollow voice, as if he'd just been lying on the bare ground for a long time, and he said, "I've known you a long time. Back when I had my accident in the Rocky Mountains, you administered first aid, then disappeared the moment the ambulance arrived. Later I saw you again, swimming in the Black Sea, way far out; we were on a yacht with friends and thought you'd been in a shipwreck, but you signaled to us to sail on; you had a cloth tied around your head just like this one. You're in the government here, behind the scenes; you pull strings."

And when the man at the wheel didn't reply, the retired poet in the back seat picked up where the other left off—as they went into the next tunnel under the Alpine foothills, or the Alps themselves—in accented German, which he seemed to exaggerate on purpose, to make people pay more attention, and said, "You and I are the same age, but you remind me of my father. You have the same genial nature as him, and the preoccupied air, which he would suddenly shake off when I disturbed him, and beat me. And like him you have several other children and are a good father to all of them. And you're lonely, and it's your own fault—wretchedly"—(or did he say "retchingly"?)—"lonely. Yes, how quickly a person can become isolated, in the time it takes to open a door, close a window, turn onto a side road."

The driver, who couldn't say anything and wouldn't have wanted to anyway, honked the horn. But even that sound came out rather feeble.

Only one thing was clear: All three of them were free and had time, at least for the next few days. A holiday was in the offing, the feast of the Ascension, which meant a long weekend.

But that applied only to him. Apparently his two passengers had no obligations, from now to the ends of their lives, whether distant or imminent. They had neither work nor family, and this was no recent development. Yet they had money, or acted as though they did, not only playing with bundles of banknotes but also flashing their credit cards. What they showed off had certainly not been acquired very honestly. But no one cared, and on the other hand, it didn't seem especially dirty, either, didn't come from drugs, or from pimping—although the two of them certainly appeared capable of the latter, especially since the names they mentioned were almost all women's, foreign ones. They both seemed rather like desperadoes, though polite ones, and at certain moments overly polite ones.

The thing the poet had spread out to dry and kept sniffing wasn't his notebook, but rather a deck of poker cards. The former Olympian was hacking away with a jackknife at the loose threads on his trouser cuffs. At the same time both were sucking peppermints, so as not to reek of the root cellar's wine as they talked; upon climbing into the car, both had almost automatically stubbed out the cigarettes they'd just lit.

They didn't take on the air of desperadoes until after the drive began, with the departure from the immediate area: open, caved-in mouths, as if prematurely toothless; a jitteriness as if they'd just escaped from some authority that had been oppressing them for too long, or from an aged mother or aunt who had been loyally taking care of them; a confusion about where to go, but in their aimlessness a death-defying energy; a sort of idiotic pleasure in the most fleeting moments and tiniest trivia, in the feeling of being on the road, such as you otherwise see only in mongoloids; at the same time, as if they were not merely lawless but also above all laws, could walk through walls and on water, could fly, could make themselves invisible, and permit themselves any misdeed you could name—because of who they were.

He briefly imagined it was these two who had struck him on the head in the woods beyond the airport, and he was now their prisoner.

Suddenly a small bird was fluttering around inside the car, a sparrow. The poet had found it somewhere, and, thinking it was dead, had stuck it in his pocket, from which it had now escaped. They stopped by the side of the road and each of them rolled down his window.

That happened past midnight, in a valley high in the inner Alps, after they'd driven over several passes, and here the rain was accompanied by lightning and thunder, lightning and thunder. The sparrow promptly flew off, its peeping actually more a piercing cry; as if this confinement, like being buried alive, had lasted much longer than just a few hours.

The skier knew a house nearby where they could spend the night. A woman lived there, "a winner, almost like me when I was younger, but in another specialty," which, however, he didn't want to name. Then, too, no one asked him, either, as if not asking questions were one of the unspoken rules of the game since they'd set out together.

As they tried to find the way—the driver, although he'd never been there before, had a clearer sense of where to go than the athlete, who allegedly knew the area; at an intersection where many roads came together, he very confidently turned in the only right direction—the poet in the back seat announced a sort of plan for the following day: "First over the border. I know a village there that's celebrating its annual festival tomorrow. Besides, an out-of-wedlock child of mine lives there—the only children I have are out-of-wedlock—whom I've never seen. The child doesn't want to see me, or at least not anymore. And then on, if possible, down the southern slope of the Alps, and up the next mountain chain, not as high, but where it can snow even now, in the summer, and where, in a forest up there, among flowers and ferns, there's a deep hole, a shaft going straight down into the earth, which is filled all year long with ice, and when you thaw a piece of it—but you'll see; I want it to be a surprise."

The woman's house lay just over the top of the hill that acted as a watershed for the area. The water from springs on one side flowed toward the Black Sea, and water on the other side toward the Mediterranean (or so the woman asserted), and two such springs, to the left and right of the divide, were brought together in a fountain that had two pipes and two basins, from which the water flowed in its appointed directions, east and south.

After their coming over the crown of the hill on this all-encircling, deep rainy night, suddenly the house in this isolated spot, far from any settlement, appeared as a house of light, a low but sprawling building of undressed stone, with not only the lanterns on both sides of the portal lit, but also the lights in all the rooms, dimmed in one wing, shining at full strength in the other, every corner brightly illuminated, even the ceilings bathed in rays as bright as the sun's. The many silhouettes seemed at first to be flitting and zigzagging back and forth between these individual rooms, as if through wide-open doors, creating the impression of a great dance, though without music, indeed without any sound at all other than the twofold gurgling of the watershed fountain outside.

It turned out that they had come to a house of mourning. The husband there had just died and had been buried the day before, and his wife, the "winner," was busy clearing out his part of the house, helped only by a distant neighbor; the speed with which they were going about it, the carefully coordinated movements they were carrying out, and the abundance of light, which multiplied their shadows: all created the impression of a house full of people.

No one, and not only he, spoke another word before bedtime. They were all very tired. Each of the three was given a room, in an annex. He heard the poet and the athlete talking a bit in the corridor, in very calm, also calming voices, like those of the two watershed springs outdoors, and he fell asleep immediately, just as he always did. And unlike his half-unused bed at home, this was the kind of bed he liked, narrow, in a very small chamber (that, too, delightfully different from home).

In that deep, soundless mountain night—even the gurgling of the watershed fountain seemed to have receded beyond the horizons—he awoke, or rather was wakened—because the light went on in the room, or rather flashed on, all the lights at once.

The woman was standing by his bed, her back very straight, wearing a heavy coat and with wet hair, as if she'd come a considerable distance, not just over from the main house. She went down on her knees before him. At the same time her face was turned in an entirely different direction, toward the room's one window, which stood wide open. (Had she climbed in this way?) And her features displayed a surprising tranquillity, most unusual, and not just for her, the so-called champion, and not only in contrast to the expression of proud, unapproachable sorrow she had worn earlier that evening. Or was this thing in her eyes actually a sort of trance? Or even transfiguration?

He remained motionless, waiting. What would the woman do? For it was clear she would do something, and at once. And in the very next moment she threw herself on him and began to pound him. She beat him violently, left, right, with both fists, and she had big hands, which she clenched into fists like a man's. And all the while she kept her eyes averted from him.

He put up no defense, and it was as if the blows hurt less that way and he remained completely unharmed. And nevertheless she was beating him with such force that eventually he fell out of his narrow bed. And only then did she let up, favor him for the first time with a brief glance, turn off the light, and disappear as she had come—somehow or other.

He climbed, or rather fell, back onto his mountain-night bed, and promptly went to sleep again, in an act of obedience, as it were. Then laughter. Had he laughed himself, in a dream? "I haven't laughed that way in a long time!" was his thought, on the verge of consciousness, but for that reason all the clearer and more memorable. And: "Not even in school did I get beaten as much as today and yesterday!"

A smell lingered in the room, not from a woman's perfume but rather from something burning, closest perhaps to the smell of two flintstones rubbed together for a long time, just before the first sparks fly. It made him breathe faster and harder, and it was a breathing that didn't seem to come just from him, but from several people crammed into the small chamber.

The next morning was also the first time—in how long?—that he didn't sit down to breakfast alone. The poet and the former Olympic champion were already waiting for him over in the main house, at a table set lavishly—and not only for that isolated mountain area—from which, however, the other two had not yet helped themselves, as if it were up to him to give the signal to begin.

It was the poet, incidentally—he let his athlete friend report this—who'd rounded up and prepared the essentials and the extras, even coffee from the hills of Jamaica, and had also gone out into the mountain forest at the crack of dawn to bring back brimming bowls of blueberries, blackberries, or huckleberries, still glistening from the rain. "For our last journey," he commented. To whom was he referring when he said "our"? Did it include him, "our driver," as the two called him at one point, or, at another, "our guest" or "the third in our group"?

One way or the other, neither of the two seemed to have noticed that he hadn't said a single word the entire time. Or it didn't matter to them, any more than the fact that overnight the wound on his forehead had been joined by others on his face—on his cheekbone, on his lips, on his cheeks—the latter probably scratched by the widow's wedding ring. They seemed preoccupied exclusively with themselves, with their own degeneration, under way for years now. And at the same time it buoyed them up, at least during the moments when they were talking about it.

During the night the poet had heard his own obituary being broadcast over the dream radio. "It was read by a woman, a radio announcer who otherwise enjoyed immense popularity for her voice, which was warm and sincere, what-ever the occasion. But in my case she sounded not merely indifferent but downright exultant, even vengeful. It was as if my death had eliminated a despised evildoer, had felled an enemy of mankind. Everything I'd written in the course of my life she dismissed, and apparently in the name of everyone else, and irrevocably, as worthless trifles. Worthless trifles! And then it was precisely this expression that put things in per-spective for me. Justifiably forgotten! she said, and suddenly I no longer saw myself as alone at all, or at least as tangibly less isolated than in previous dreams and days. A succession of fail-ures and defeats! said the radio lady, and I saw myself grin-ning in my sleep, from ear to ear. Just wait, I thought, I haven't even written my book yet. And it will be a book unlike any before it, not tangible as a book, not forcing its way into the picture, nothing you get hold of, weightless, and yet a book—

if ever there was one. The bush for it is already burning. Or it'll take place in a realm beyond all burning bushes, Jacob's ladders, and descents to hell."

He laughed over his whole face—or was it only almost?—and then counted his money—if that was all he had, he wouldn't get far—while the former national champion at his side, likewise sorting his rather meager banknotes and the coins as well—among the latter a cheap metal reproduction of the gold medal he'd long since pawned—recounted how, after his winning days as a skier were over, he'd tried just about every other sport, thinking no athletic discipline was off limits to him, and indeed that anything he undertook would have to bring him victories.

"That was true, at least for a while, but the price I had to pay was that little, then less and less, was at stake or was required for winning. I won a whole succession of motorcross races, but my competitors were mostly weekend athletes, and in the end I was winning on routes out beyond the most remote villages. And after that, in all my other athletic attempts, I could win, or at least imagine winning, only by going abroad, or rather disappearing, to more and more distant destinations, to the most foreign of foreign lands. As a 'foreign competitor' I had, if not success, at least an aura, as I'd once had in my homeland as a 'grand champion.' So I was the star player on a Korean basketball team for a season, and the following year went to a medium-sized city in New Zealand as both player and coach to establish European football there—and I was popular for that for a while—then shone in golf tournaments in Mongolia and in ice hockey in

Fairbanks, Alaska. But in the end my only way out was to go home, to get a job or start a business of my own. Except that winning was so much in my blood that even here, in an entirely different kind of competition, I expected it, expected to have it handed to me. I demanded it. Out of the way, the rest of you, you also-rans. There's nothing here for you. I have to be the champion. I'm the champion—who else? And so for the last ten years it's been one disaster after another, and each more ruinous than the last. So this is my last journey. But who knows, maybe with the help of our fine driver here, it'll turn into my first? A productive detour? Off to a foreign country where I can finally win something again!"

And then he had laughed all over his face, and raised his arms in the victory gesture; but he, too, didn't quite carry it off; and the tongue he stuck out as he cheered looked white from an exhaustion that wasn't merely physical.

It was still raining, and with every moment that passed the rain seemed to come down even harder, or more concentratedly. Water came shooting, squirting, spitting from the two pipes in the watershed fountain, hastening toward one sea here, the antipodal one there, and all the larches in the mountain forest, their fine needles—in contrast to the coarser ones of the spruces—long since unable to mount resistance to the wetness pounding down, stood there as if in a waterworks.

Not a trace of the woman anywhere in the house. Or had the fire in the tiled stove been lit by her, in the middle of summer? And then, as he escorted the two others to the car under a giant umbrella, which seemed to have been put there for them in the door to the courtyard, the person simply referred to as "driver" felt something rustling in his jacket pocket that made him think involuntarily of a letter "sewn into the lining."

At the wheel, the journey under way again, the recurring question: What was it he'd been missing all morning: his house? his familiar surroundings? the way to work? No. It was something he'd neglected, failed to do. Take a necessary medication? No, that wasn't it, either—it had to do with a form of nourishment he was lacking, without actually feeling weak, some tonic. But hadn't they had a good breakfast, and only good, wholesome stuff, as they said?

And yet there was something missing, or rather that emptiness you feel tickling your mouth, for instance when you have an apple or a piece of bread set aside and then don't get around to eating it—except that the sense of missing something wasn't localized in his mouth, but where? in his entire body? his whole person. The book! Right, this morning he hadn't read anything in his book, the medieval epic, and thus he was missing something like his "breakfast." A pharmacist who was a voracious reader—did such a thing exist? (And this was the last time, at least for the time when his story takes place, that he thought of himself as the "pharmacist.")

The poet, in the passenger seat, was just reading his horoscope out loud from the newspaper; it predicted that on this particular day he would be overtaken by a feeling of "incurable loneliness," but there was no call for despair if he remained open to the possibilities lying right before his eyes—such an attitude could be the "cure." No, it wasn't this reading his organism had been feeling the lack of—and besides, the veteran athlete in the back seat now pointed out to the poet that the newspaper was a year old.

Momentarily it seemed to the driver as if everything he was experiencing just then and everything that had happened with him and the others since the previous evening, were being simultaneously recorded and could be read somewhere, though in neither a newspaper nor a book. Hadn't he already had some such a notion at one time or another in the past? Yes, in certain hours of love, of great happiness or great unhappiness, with his wife—was all that still true?—with his children—was all that still true?—with his mistress—long, long ago, or perhaps never? And in each case that image of simultaneous recording had turned up only in the depths of night, in the complete absence of any sound, as if no one were breathing. And now his current story was offering itself for reading in broad daylight, with rain pounding on the roof of the car, with his passengers coughing, scratching themselves, yawning.

He uncharacteristically stepped on the gas, even on this serpentine back road in the mountains, still far from any pavement, and added a quick curve of his own, thereby missing, without particularly meaning to, the boulder that unexpectedly hurtled onto the road.

He alone glimpsed for a second their hostess of the night before, high up on an overhang, her back already turned to the scene of the crime. The two others had merely stopped their scratching and yawning for the instant, only to go back to yawning and scratching with a vengeance.

And this wasn't the first time he realized that since a particular moment he'd been in mortal danger, indeed in imminent danger, like that just now, and also in entirely different,
unforeseeable ways.

It was here, however, that he made up his mind—unlike the
last few times when he'd landed in such situations—that he
would keep his eyes and nostrils as wide open and for as long as
possible, at the same time waging the struggle to survive, and
would become a constant witness, phase by phase, to whatever
was threatening him, was closing in on his body or his soul—no,
even more, and beyond that: to keep all his senses alert to everything else, while this mortal danger was close, always close by;
along with the main things and those accompanying them, to
impress on himself the ephemera as well, the unconnected
things, things taking place somewhere else entirely, so to
speak—or rather, to incorporate them into himself, with all his
senses, perhaps also (yet that wasn't the reason) as a way out.

The few times in the past when things "had closed in"—
when he'd lost his way while climbing in the mountains, got
stuck in a seemingly impenetrable tangle of brambles—he'd
always managed to find his way out again, simply by instinct,
surefootedly and -handedly, but at the same time blindly, deaf
from the pounding of the blood in his ears, had found his way
out like someone in danger of drowning who doesn't flail
futilely but swims purposefully toward land, yet in the process
takes in: nothing, nothing at all.

His first such experience had been in childhood, during
the flight at the end of the war with his parents, in the
predawn gray, across the mined border: Not even now, long

after the event, did any image come to him, unless it was that of the gray before dawn, a cold grayness without a breath of air, and indeed without any atmosphere, which didn't dissipate or come to an end; surely there had been pursuers, "on their heels," but he hadn't seen them, didn't see them.

But now, in the moment of evading the stone, he opened his eyes and saw, not only out of their corners, next to the woman up there, an effect born of the combination of pouring rain and a pale sun breaking through, something like her shade or double, and above their heads the cloudy sky. He, and with him all the others, were less in a tight spot here than in the midst of the action; in a sphere. Yes, it was one, albeit a strange one. And if the woman hadn't had her back turned, he would have given her a sign then and there, any sign.

At the time when this story takes place, wherever even a remote trail, such as the one they found themselves on, met a main road, however deserted, the intersection was structured as a roundabout, and this was true all over the continent.

And this circling continued on the highway, and occurred even more often here because there were correspondingly larger numbers of roads feeding into each other. Just when you'd got somewhat accustomed to the straightaway and were imagining you could make headway toward your destination at last, or at least move ahead unimpeded, you came upon another roundabout, and then another, and so forth.

And at the end of such a journey, even one lasting for days, you could find that you had no sense of the direction in which you'd been traveling, or sense of having traveled at all.

Indeed, your head might be spinning, as after too long a ride, which also seems to end up at almost the same spot where it started, even when it lets you off in an entirely different country.

Arriving this way at a presumably distant destination could leave you not only dizzy but also fed up with travel altogether or even with just setting out, travel-sick—which was even worse than seasick—and filled with disgust at any movement whatsoever from place to place.

At the time when this story takes place, it had reached the point that you could hardly get to the tops of mountain passes by car anymore. Most of the passes in Europe were out of service, so to speak, and for the most part also rendered impassable by uncleared rock slides, washouts, and the like. Instead of crossing the continent above ground by way of the passes, people traveled almost exclusively underground through tunnels, of which by now there were as many on some stretches as roundabouts on others. Although the number of national borders had increased—there were more than ever before, often coming in the middle of such tunnels—these went unnoticed, since all border controls had been eliminated, and a border guard was nowhere to be seen.

Having these tunnels under this part of the world helped make any long trip seem like a ride through a chamber of horrors, a ride where the end seemed to be right back at the beginning. Having set out on an adventure in a foreign country, you found yourself on your own doorstep, with even the same knocker and a similar monogram on the doormat, or at least on a street almost identical to the familiar one at home, whether in a city, a suburb, or the country: out of the tunnel and promptly back home—even if you'd planned never to return.

On this particular day, the three of them had a different experience, however. True, they stopped and circled in thousands of roundabouts, rond-points, rotundas, and turnabouts, and rolled through about five hundred tunnels—some shorter, some longer—coming to a standstill time and again among millions of holiday cars. But their mood, and more particularly their condition, internal as well as external, proved stronger than all these circumstances.

Each of them was in a different mood: With the poet, it was primarily nervousness, because he'd be seeing his almost unknown child—"I'm less nervous about the mother"; with the former Olympic medalist it was perhaps curiosity as to whether in this foreign country—recently become a "skiing nation" (but also a "football" and "sprinter nation")—his name still carried weight; with the chauffeur it was a strange yearning, such as he had felt only in what he saw as his much too short youth, together with an unaccustomed sadness.

What they shared, however, was their condition, or their consciousness: of an adventure, dangerous in some unspecified way, one in which a great deal, indeed everything, was at stake, an adventure, furthermore, on the verge of the forbidden, the illegal, even of a criminal offense. Against the law? Against the way of the world? And none of them could have said where this shared consciousness came from. In any case, what they were doing, or especially would be doing in the future, could bring punishment down on their heads, a punishment without mercy. But turning back now was out of the question for them.

And accordingly, in spite of everything, they really experienced their journey as something new and unprecedented.

He drove fairly slowly. He'd never been on good terms with speed, in any case, had never succeeded in jumping onto the speed train.

The few times he'd been on an airplane, he'd thought the speed would do him in, especially during take-off, when it could be felt most acutely. After the first time, he'd shied away from window seats—though that didn't help much: The speed affected not only his eyes but also his whole body. It would destroy him now, right now.

And this had come over him very early on, long before his first flight. At a certain speed it wasn't just that he didn't know whether he was coming or going. Even on a bicycle he would lose—from one moment to the next—all control over his body, and a fall would become inevitable. It had taken several concussions for him to recognize that these accidents out of the clear blue sky weren't the fault of a particular bicycle, the road, or his clumsiness. Just as other people were claustrophobic, agoraphobic, or acrophobic, he was afflicted with what might be called tachophobia, or fear of speed, actually a kind of panic attack—when a certain, or rather an uncertain speed was reached—that would suddenly throw off his equilibrium.

The only automobile accident he'd ever had had come about in just this way; he'd been engrossed in conversation with someone in the passenger seat and had inadvertently exceeded his personal speed limit, hardly noticeably, by only a little—yet all at once he'd been unable to keep hold of the steering wheel, and bang! it had happened. (It was good, at least in the present situation, that he was still mute, and instead of speaking, just mused to himself or listened to the others in the car, something that had hardly ever caused him to speed up.)

"Even as an observer, as an outsider," he told me, "I could fall prey to some speeds. But they had to reach a specific point, for example at a Formula One race that I watched one time outdoors, not on television, on the urging of my wife, who was always crazy for speed and bloomed in its presence as nowhere else, and displayed all her beauty—a wondrously beautiful and, to me, sometimes terrifyingly beautiful speed demon—or another time at the Hahnenkamm, the most famous downhill skiing competition of that winter, and that time, too, I'd gone to Kitzbühel for her sake, to observe the champions live for a change. And when the race cars appeared, and she broke out in cheers—I don't remember whether it was in the Eifel or in Estoril, atop the volcano or along the Atlantic cliffs—the sight literally made me stagger backward, and I had to hold onto something, because these drivers came racing along unbelievably fast, immeasurably faster than on television—unnaturally fast? no, superterrestrially fast. One minute they were there, the next minute it was as if they'd never been there. And my wife and I let out a cry at the same moment, but hers was a cry of delight, mine one of fright, of a sort of primal terror."

And the downhill ski race on the Kitzbühel piste affected him much the same: As the first contestant zoomed into sight up above, emerging from a patch of woods onto the long, precipitous descent, at an extraplanetary or at least inhuman speed, the sight hit him like a blow on the head—although, in contrast to the racing cars, this filled him with enthusiasm, as it did his wife, except that this time he didn't cry out, but instead couldn't utter a word for quite a while. "So it started that long ago, then?" I said. — "Yes and it wasn't the first time."

And the former skiing champion in the back seat of the car—hadn't he been the Hahnenkamm winner that time?—now remarked, more to himself but also as if he'd been reading the driver's thoughts and were answering him: "Exposing yourself to speed is essential. If you don't pull it off, you're unequipped for living, and that's nothing new. I think I didn't get out of diapers and become my own man until the moment I deliberately committed myself to speed, or deliberately let the highest speeds possible have their way with me. They cured me of my Why-me? and Why-always-me? existence, without making me any less myself. I felt at home with these speeds. Maybe what's finished me is that I'm not so fast anymore." (Burst of laughter.)

Yes, it seemed to be fine with the other two that he was driving rather unhurriedly. They had time. At least that was the phrase that was repeated over and over, like a mantra. "We have time," the poet said in the middle of one of those Trans-Europe Tunnel traffic jams: "I've heard the village festival

we're on our way to lasts for several days, and anyway, it's supposed to take place mainly at night."

They had time, and stopped fairly frequently at one of the
generic European roadside eating places, though no matter
what they ordered, they always ate standing up. They had time,
and at one roundabout they turned off onto a dirt road, got out,
and let themselves be rained on a little—the driver stayed in
the car. They traipsed through quite a few filling-station shops,
purchasing various trifles, and showing off to the driver, who
went in with them, how many languages they spoke.

The rain didn't let up. The light changed. One time a car
passed them so fast that their driver almost snapped the steering wheel in two. Wasn't it the woman from the previous
evening, racing by in a Santana? It occurred to him that he'd
never seen her head on, even during the blows she'd administered, but only in profile, for instance when they'd reached her
house and found her standing in the doorway, in the guise of
the unapproachable grieving widow.

The last tunnel was even longer than usual. Yet the other side,
which they were supposed to reach eventually, could be
glimpsed from far off, at first as small as if you were looking
through a piece of paper rolled up as tightly as possible, or
through the tiny knothole in a barn wall, or through the dot-
sized gap in your own fist.

He drove even slower. The tunnel road was so straight he
hardly had to pay attention to steering. In this way the end
of the tunnel remained constantly in the picture, growing

almost imperceptibly larger. For a while it actually looked rather like a picture—that's how one-dimensional the image appeared, a light pinprick in the midst of the encompassing blackness (the tunnel wasn't lit, and he hadn't turned on the headlights, had completely forgotten to at the sight of the bright spot far in the distance, and that didn't seem to disturb anyone else in the car; all of them had eyes for only one thing).

Wasn't it perhaps an illusion that the road led into the open, way off there in the distance? The image of the tunnel exit appeared so rigid, also so artificial—including the light, which wasn't dim at all but rather bright and sunny—that in their eyes, and until shortly before they emerged, it looked like part of the subterranean gallery they were in. A miniature photographic slide, in glaring colors and overexposed, seemed to be projected onto an otherwise completely dark surface, a kind of leaf-green flickering and cliff-face reddish yellow.

And for a very long moment this sight created the impression that they weren't moving anymore, weren't budging from the spot, indeed had wandered out of space, were just being shaken a bit to preserve the illusion, and soon it would be all over—over how?—all over.

And strangely enough, the impression, or the hallucination, gained strength as the image of the tunnel exit gradually grew larger. The brilliantly colored surface moved toward them, getting bigger and bigger, but showing no movement whatsoever. Already bushes and eventually grasses, too, could be made out, seemingly overilluminated, more true to life than life, and also seemingly larger than life. Yet all these details remained motionless. Where were they? Were they still anywhere at all? Why was no one else driving through the tunnel? Why wasn't there a single car in the opposite direction?

And now the hole already took up almost the entire surface, just as motionlessly colorful as at the beginning. "Evil passage," he remembered, had been a term in the old epics for a struggle ending in almost certain death. And at the same time this was splendid. To his surprise, he saw no harm, just as earlier that morning, in speeding up. Onward and inward!

And only now, just a few turns of the wheels, it seemed, before their being swallowed up, did the images of blistering yellow cliffs draw apart, while the grassy and leafy surfaces on all sides began to move, as if released from a spell—which had perhaps not been so evil, after all? For in the moment of the car's leaving the tunnel, wherever they looked, the trees, including the largest trunks, were moving all the more freely, positively frenetically, and how three-dimensional the cliffs appeared out here on either side of the road, which itself suddenly looked three-dimensional, too; yes, indeed, how much space the cliffs gave the new arrivals.

One of them even clapped, the way people do upon landing after a transoceanic flight in an unexpectedly beautiful and especially promising place. A new day had begun upon their leaving the tunnel, or could now begin, also thanks to this tunnel here. Curious adventure. A modern adventure?

At any rate, from this moment on, their attention was focused on the festival they were now approaching. They were looking forward to it. The driver, too, the stranger, the third party, whom the others didn't even bother to ask?

"Yes, I, too, suddenly felt, and for the first time in ages, in a party mood," he told me. "And that emergence from the hole was also the first time during that trip that I thought of the poet, the Olympic medalist, and myself as 'we.' We were looking forward to what was in store for us. But after that I wasn't able to think in terms of a 'we' like that very often."

As for the outward circumstances, the new day was already over after just a few more turns of the wheels and perhaps a single blink. It was only the tunnel opening that had made what lay ahead appear as bright as day, even as bright as the sun, with apparent burning intensity.

In reality dusk was falling. To be sure, it wasn't raining here, and hadn't rained either. The sky was cloudless, high. Curious that it already seemed autumnal, indeed almost wintry. Perhaps because the whole landscape was at a higher elevation, was a plateau?

In fact, the road was crowded with trucks and tractors carrying full loads of firewood, and the isolated houses along the way had woodpiles reaching up to their windows, surrounding the windows, stacked up to the eaves. And what were all these utility vehicles doing on the roads? Wasn't today a feast day, and a special one in this region, the major feast day of the year?

The poet didn't know the way, and not for the first time on this journey; he'd never come to the village by car.

Besides, the name of the village had slipped his mind. All he knew was that it was a name with resonance, a famous one, but only the name, not the village. It merely bore the name of a world-famous town, had been named for it. Or was it the other way around, and the town in question had been named after the village eons ago, and perhaps the village's name was the original one? Or did innumerable settlements exist, independent of one another, all over the world, with the same name, conferred because of their particular location, because of a common patron saint, or simply because of the sound, and one of them had then become the one everyone talked about?

"What *is* the name of the town where my child lives? Belo Horizonte? Alexandria? Lodi? Bethlehem? San Sebastian? Santiago? Fort Apache? It could even be something like Manila or Danzig!"

And although he described the village down to the smallest detail—above all in such detail, and that seemed to be where the poet was in his element—to the athlete, who'd already been all over the world, the athlete couldn't help him either. In that broad, rather undifferentiated rocky landscape, all the settlements resembled each other, at least in the eyes of someone like the athlete, who had passed through there only once, and now, with night coming on, they seemed even a shade more alike, and besides, in the past the competitive champion hadn't been paying attention to the small features the poet described in such an odd state of excitement.

And something else: many, indeed almost every town marker they drove by—and soon they were lit up—displayed the name of a well-known town, for the most part a large one, or at least closely resembled a famous one, and could at first be mistaken for it. Except that, after such promissory signs, fulfillment never followed, or at least so it seemed on first impression (but on second impression there was nothing left of the specific village in any case), and the poet just shook his head guiltily each time.

Thus they passed through St. Quentin, Löwen, Santo Domingo, Venice, Ragusa, Pireos (sic!), Jeruzalem (sic!), Rangun, Fährbank, the scatter-settlements or hamlets of Rosental, Troy, Jerico, Pompey, Heiliggrab/San Sepulcro, Monterey/Königsberg—bilingual signs—Leiden, Bethel, Dallas, Lustenau, Liebenau, Valparaiso, Boston, and even passed a signpost that read "Taxham" (so there were at least two of them in the world!).

The driver up front had long since ceased slowing down at any of the signs, no longer turned inquiringly to the poet, after a while simply drove right by all the villages, drove with increasing confidence, as if he were perfectly sure of where he was going.

And in fact, during the one and only stop they made, outside "St. Quentin," he had slipped out the letter sewn into his suit, without anyone's noticing, had opened it and cast a quick glance at it, without actually reading it for the time being. There was a sketch included, with their destination clearly marked, along with its name, and unmistakable arrows showing where they had to turn off.

Ridiculous or not: the village, or whatever it was, was called "Santa Fe," one of perhaps thousands on all continents (surely there was one even in Australia, or in Asia, on Goa, or near Macao?).

Of course, they could also have listened for sounds coming from a festival or looked out for cascades of light in the rock-and-steppe-scape, so easy to take in as a whole, and where, when you stopped and listened, even small sounds carried a great distance. Yet once the trucks with firewood had disappeared at quitting time, it had soon turned out that there was hardly a village in the region that didn't have its own special festival under way on this particular day; even at an intersection with only two or three houses, a tent had been pitched next to them, leaving these flat structures in the shadows, such was the din, smoke, steam, and stamping emanating from it.

"And it must be said," the "driver" told me, "that at first we stopped now and then not so much to ask directions as to join the action, the dancing, singing, and playing—at least that was true of the athlete and the poet fellow. Pretty remarkable, how enterprising these two allegedly lost souls could be: the way one of them jumped into the dance without a moment's hesitation, yet wasn't looked at askance or as an interloper or stranger by anyone. And the way the other fell in with a procession as if it were completely natural, and even seized one pole of the canopy under which the statue of the Blessed Virgin was being carried. The way one of them was no sooner out of the car than he was participating in the bow-and-arrow contest already under way, and won a bottle of wine. And the way the other likewise picked up an instrument lying idle and played it, applauded even by the musician to whom it belonged, when he returned from his break. And the curious thing was that in every case the one could also have been the other. That surprised me most with the poet. On the other hand, I had meanwhile long since forgotten that he even was any such thing. And it seemed to me then that I was the only one of us who felt urgency about reaching our destination."

At first the poet didn't recognize this "Santa Fe," despite the steep ridge on which it perches, carved out by two rivers that converge there, and thus very distinct from all the other clusters of houses in that part of the country. Finally, while they were still down below, at a ramshackle, overgrown railroad station, the headlights picked out an oval enameled sign indicating the place's altitude above sea level—almost a thousand meters "above the Mediterranean"—and he exclaimed: "This is it! We're there!" but then surprisingly fell silent, and probably not only because even now he didn't know which way to go to find his former lover and the child.

Throughout the town—no, it wasn't a village—in the lower as well as the upper portion, festival sites turned up. The sketched map even contained the name of the street or alley where they were supposed to go. The driver wordlessly showed it to the poet, with the letter part folded back, and he registered no surprise.

None of the passersby they asked could help them. Were they strangers here themselves? No, but at the time when this story takes place, most of the local inhabitants and long-time residents hardly knew their way around anymore, hardly knew the town except for their own immediate neighborhoods. At first it seemed as though all the people they approached for information were travelers, too, in fact from the same country as those who were asking them. The reason was this: As soon as the car windows were rolled down, they heard, from those standing around outside celebrating, mostly in larger groups, something like their familiar German language, even Austrian dialect. But no, it was an entirely different idiom after all, that of this Santa Fe (the two passengers vied with one another in speaking to the people on the street to prove their mastery of it)—and had all languages in the meantime come to sound so similar at a distance?

Also from nearby, the phrases and flourishes had an international flavor, to the point that the speakers often switched roles: If the foreigners greeted them with "Hola," "Buenas noches," "Adiós," "Gracias," they were answered with "Hallo," "Hi," "Guten Tag," "Tschüs," "Ciao," "You're welcome," "Servus," "Auf Wiedersehen." To match, one neon sign read "Mozart" (a video arcade), another "Tyrol" (a bed-and-breakfast without breakfast), the third "Mainz" (a nightclub tiled in Moorish-Andalusian style). And from a steep alley, barely the width of a man's shoulders and otherwise pitch black, through which people had perhaps once been dragged to the local Inquisition stake, signs flashed for "Gösser Bier" or "Hahnen Alt," with the appropriate advertising slogans, they, too, all in German.

Had they ever left the city of Salzburg? Illuminated, along with its looming, naked, vertically plummeting cliff, by a generic European, cold piercing light, mightn't the old part of town here have just as well been the fortress from there?—But no, they were completely and utterly here, in this Santa Fe, as particular as it was unique, away from Salzburg, away from Taxham, far, far in the distance, which you could already sense from the different sky, and especially from the nocturnal wind wafting in through the car's windows, now always open.

"In the distance": who determined such a thing? To some extent, as was already noted, it was they themselves, their mood and their circumstances, their situation, and then it was the story, the tale; the fact they knew that they were on a journey together in a story. So the awareness of experiencing a story, and a shared one, too, created a sense of distance, even if they might not have set out from home?

"Does this happen to you sometimes, too," the pharmacist of Taxham asked me long afterward: "Suddenly you stumble upon something you've been looking for in vain for a long time? That's how it worked out for me the evening we arrived in Santa Fe. All at once, after extended roaming around, back and forth through the town, I realized where people were expecting us, supposedly. I didn't even realize it consciously, wouldn't have been able to express it; but from one moment to the next I struck out for the place, without the slightest hesitation, guided by the moon, by an unfamiliar constellation, or simply by the nocturnal wind, which I let blow in our faces. And from that another name came to me for this probably somewhat misleading, disturbing, or deceptive Santa Fe in my story: Town of the Nocturnal Wind. And that's what I'd like to call it from now on in this account. And then we got to the street we were looking for and went straight to the right house."

"Here we are!" the poet exclaimed, again not surprised at the driver, and as if he himself had guided them there: "That's the brick missing from the wall, and inside the hole's still the little bird's hiding place!"—And the athlete in back said, "Yes, that's exactly where it is, the sparrow's niche in the hole in the wall"—as if he were an expert on the area and had even spent his childhood on this street.

That night it was almost impossible to make out anything about the street—where it was located and where it led. True, it had extra lighting for the festival—powerful streetlights and spotlights, most of them shining from houses or garages, which were opened as wide as possible, but the lights were only here and there, so that the long stretches in between seemed even darker.

At first you were blinded, as was also the case outside the house in question. The driver guessed the presence of an even longer dark stretch at the end of the street, after which there were no more lights and the street didn't continue but merged with—what? At any rate, here they weren't in the upper town, where the entire surrounding area would have been lit as bright as day, or rather as brightly as a stage.

And even though on his hands and also everywhere else on himself he could still make out the residual smells from home, from before their departure, and could have differentiated them all, named and narrated them—smells from specific rooms, from the garden, from the airport forest, from the root-cellar restaurant, from the border-marking river that still clung to him from swimming—now the nocturnal wind from that darkness at the end of the street wafted a smell past his nose that he at first took for happiness. And he was amazed. "But," he told me later, "on the few occasions when there was any suggestion of my being happy, it was always as if I were getting above myself. And punishment always followed swiftly."

Shading their eyes with their hands, the three looked around the street festival. The door they were seeking was closed, the only one on the street that was. What appeared to be many lights inside was merely the reflection of those outside. Otherwise the building matched the others—long and low to the ground, no higher than a hut, it blended seamlessly with the houses to its right and left, and, white-stuccoed like them, formed an unbroken row. True, smoke was puffing from the chimney, from a wood fire. The customary curtain of glass or metal beads was missing from the doorway, and there was no doorbell.

The poet seemed in no hurry to knock and enter. It was as if he were waiting to make a grand entrance on the street, with the other two as his entourage. But although he'd spent several years here, and supposedly had also been a celebrity in these parts, no one recognized him anymore, or they overlooked him (even when he drew attention to himself, as now, he wasn't conspicuous). At most, someone might be taken aback for a moment, but then didn't know what to do with him. Nor did he recognize anyone. "They've all moved away," he said. One time he was about to greet a former neighbor, and it was the neighbor's son, who even when the poet introduced himself and provided some unmistakable information about himself, the former neighbor, and the history of the street, remained a stranger, as much a stranger as a person can be to anyone.

"Nothing gets passed down anymore," he said, and then, when it happened again, and the person he took for a former neighbor turned out to be her granddaughter, "What time am I living in? Have I completely lost track of time?"

No one at the street festival recognized the former Olympic champion, but there was one obvious reason for that: Even if you'd remembered an earlier photo of him, you would never have connected it with the picture he presented now; in the quarter century since, the gold-medalist's appearance had changed so much that not a single feature in his face was the same, as if he'd had an operation, yet without a real operation; and not only his skin color but even his eye color was different, or altered; hence the shock would be all the greater if someone did recognize him, this man who in the guise of someone-or-other wasn't shocking at all: "No, it can't be you! For heaven's sake!" At any rate, the champion skier had heard this exclamation a few times in his own country. But here: no chance, or also no danger of that.

The only one of them who was spoken to in the crowd, and not just once, was the one who walked behind the other two, half in their shadow: their driver. "You were on TV recently, in a Western!" — "I know you: You're the doctor who found the cure for whatever-it-was, aren't you?" — "Hi, what brings you to our godforsaken country and our out-of-this-world region, and to this dead end of all dead-end streets?" But he, for his part, didn't respond to any of this, acted as though he didn't speak the language, and thus managed to avoid revealing the fact that he'd lost the power of speech; the poet and athlete helped him out by playing along with the mistaken identities and taking on the role of his bodyguards, interpreters, and general spokesmen.

But most of the people on that long street, which every few steps changed into another festival venue, weren't just entirely preoccupied with themselves but also served as their own stars. That was a fairly familiar phenomenon among the many young people gathered outside, and there was even something cheering, occasionally gratifying, and then endearing about this, also because of the way they traveled in packs. "The world's their oyster," the poet remarked at the sight of one such group of youths clearing themselves a path—all the others had to squeeze by them—or at the sight of a couple, both of whom were trying to find their reflection in each other's faces, and, once it was found, growing more intimate and waxing doubly or triply tender, or at the sight of a person standing alone in the semidarkness and caressing him- or herself, or allowing the nocturnal wind to do it.

"It's not true," the poet commented, "that Narcissus was in love with his own reflection. What actually happened is that he was gifted or cursed with an overwhelming love for the world. He was born and grew up filled with tenderness toward all beings and phenomena, from his fingertips to the most remote corners of the universe. Young Narcissus was the soul of devotion and affection, and wished for nothing more than to take the whole world in his arms. But the world, at least the human world, didn't permit that, recoiled from him, didn't return his loving gaze. His enthusiasm for existence and his devotion to the known and unknown alike couldn't find an anchor anywhere. And so, as time passed, he had to find an anchor in himself. And so Narcissus, that great lover of the world, clung to himself. And so he ultimately came to grief. But it was good that way after all, better that way: He could have become a world conqueror, a winner of battles, a statesman, sociologist, a preacher, a scourge of God, a prophet, the founder of a religion, a national or universal poet." — "I assume you know what you're talking about," the Olympic champion replied. — "Yes," said the poet, "and I myself never set my heart on creating something beautiful or exemplary or useful, or even immortal. Maybe that would have been the right thing for me eventually. But first and foremost I always wanted to do good, just good. Yes, do good. Except that I didn't realize this until it was too late."

It wasn't just the young people at the nocturnal street festival who took the part of protagonists. Next to one of the bonfires was an infant in its carriage who had apparently just learned to sit up and kept pointing at a lamb the adults were roasting over the fire and shouting at them, as if he were in charge

there, and at the same time he would look around the circle
of bystanders for an audience, to see whether people were
admiring him sufficiently. The priest, waiting out in front of
the church there on the street, which was hardly larger
than the houses, for the people who would attend the evening
festival Mass, was standing on a rock pushed up to the
entrance, since the little church had no steps, and scrutinizing
everyone who strolled by, and even more closely those coming
in, like the patrolman on duty. One older man with leprosy—
so they still had that here? yes!—noseless, lipless, almost ear-
less, stood on the brightest spot on the street—in the
spotlights intended for a musical group that wasn't there
yet—and kept turning his head in search of people he could
approach, not for a conversation but only for his, the faceless
one's, tirade, consisting almost entirely of obscenities: Amidst
the formless blur of his features, his sharply outlined, youth-
ful eyes sparkled all the more intensely; while next to him, in
the beam of light, an ancient madwoman danced, her face
turned up toward the night sky; anyone who tried to ignore
her she punished with a most supercilious gaze.

Thus they made their way to the end of the street. What came
after that, if anything, couldn't be made out, because of the
wall of light. Besides, the last summons to Mass was now
sounded by the church bell, actually more like a hammering
on an empty tin can suspended there, and with these few
strokes the street emptied out. Only here and there was a fire
watch left outside.

The strangers also found themselves swept along for the service. And it seemed as though the priest, now inside at the tiny little altar, dressed in his festal vestments, teetering on tiptoe as if prepared for battle, had been waiting just for them. After he'd looked searchingly at all the others—amazing how many visitors had found standing room in the church, which the hundreds of candles made even smaller—they suddenly received from him a profoundly cordial, welcoming glance.

Similarly, the people from the street seemed transformed during the celebration of the Mass, or at least each lost his noticeable and idiosyncratic features, and that for a while afterward. A picture hung above the altar, apparently painted and mounted just for the occasion, showing the ascension of the Blessed Virgin; all you could see down below were her naked feet, the soles black like a peasant woman's, and, up above, her eyes, gazing heavenward. In between was a large, colorful cloud, probably easier for an amateur to paint than the whole body.

While the poet, like most of those in the church, went up to take Communion, followed by the athlete, who simply imitated him in this, as in so many things, the third man finally had time to read the letter that had been planted on him. It read as follows: "You threw your son out in a wrongful fit of anger. As punishment, a mark grew on your forehead, from which you will die. True, it has been cut out for now. But I shall see to it that it grows back. Even if I have to strike you another ten times. Yes: have to. For it hurt me, too. And have a good night in Santa Fe, on the edge of the steppe!"

. . .

After Mass he stayed in the church a while longer. His two traveling companions had gone out to find the poet's child. And despite the aura of candles and incense and the aroma of roasting meat wafting in from the street, here that other smell, borne from far away by the nocturnal wind, again proved dominant. "I pricked up my ears," he told me, "as if smells and listening were somehow related!" And at the same time he watched two young women who were standing in a specially lit corner of the church by a statue of the dead Son of God stretched out there.

The corpse was almost naked, life-sized and in all the colors of life, yet also glazed so that each feature of the body of Christ, wrought by the sculptor with utmost delicacy, acquired a special sheen. And, as was apparently customary in the latitude of this nocturnal-wind town, the two girls now bent over this lifelike body, and kissed it from top to toe. They did so gently, almost without touching the forehead, eyes, mouth, and so on with their lips, and with their praying hands pressed to their breasts. Only at the end, when they straightened up and cast one more glance at the man stretched out there, did one of them run her hand quickly across the dead man's hips, tracing the curve there with her fingertips, then cast up her eyes at the second young woman, who eyed her back, one suddenly the spitting image of the other, eyebrows raised, both smiling with lips closed, as if they were accomplices, both in the know. And they wouldn't have been surprised if upon another such caress their supposedly dead god had suddenly begun to rouse beneath their hands.

. . .

Meanwhile, there was a reviewing stand outside for the street-festival queen with her ladies-in-waiting and pages. And here he also found his passengers.

In the minutes of growing stillness that preceded the appearance of the royal retinue, the poet again talked quietly, as if conversing with himself, and yet as if he knew the driver's thoughts and had read the menacing letter addressed to him. He said more or less the following: "Lately mutual hostility has been planted between woman and man. These days men and women are furious at each other, without exception. I, for instance, haven't had an enemy in a long time—and am no longer suitable to be one myself—but if I have one, it's a woman. It's not only that we're not loved anymore; they're fighting us. And if love enters the picture, all it does is unleash war. Sooner or later the woman who loves you will be disappointed, in one way or another, and you won't even know why. She's seen through you, she'll explain, but without telling you in what respect. And she won't let you forget for a minute that you've been seen through. For at the same time she'll hardly ever leave you alone, or at any rate far less than before in lovemaking. And with her constantly there, you can hardly get away from the bad opinion she has of you. Of course, you don't think of yourself as a swindler, liar, and cheat, and would still like to be a good man in her eyes, as in the beginning. But you're forced to see yourself as all that and worse: in and with her eyes, which from now on won't let you go, and in which, no matter what you do or don't do, you'll find confirmation of her bad opinion, her bitter disappointment. Try as you will: You are and will remain the one who's been seen through. Nothing about you can surprise the woman now. Even if you manage to fulfill her most secret dreams and wishes in life, she'll merely raise her eyebrows as her gaze comes to rest on you. And if you die for her, she'll still be there bending over you, thereby keeping you from seeing anything else, even in your last seconds. Yes, nowadays hatred is the lot of man and woman from the beginning. Never was there as much filth and contamination between the sexes as there is today. And the only ones who aren't filthy are the stupid ones. Maybe that was always the case. But if so, certainly never so blatantly and so nakedly. Did we use to suffer each other in silence? And perhaps what we have now is better? At any rate, it's happening all over, not just to me and you. There's not a single couple, whether touchingly young or old and dignified, that couldn't suddenly experience an outbreak of dissension in some situation or other, and that happens today without exception—even if it gets covered up afterward—dissension for which the potential existed between woman and man from the beginning, at least in our own era. And in that case it's better to hit each other immediately, the first time you meet, don't you think? Instead of a penetrating look, instead of blushing and going pale, instead of feeling a stab in the heart, you should go at each other tooth and nail, don't you think? And why don't modern men and women leave one another in peace—at least for a while? I, at least, have been left in peace for a long time now."

. . .

Then they sat at one of the long outdoor tables and dined with the residents from the street. And at last the royal entourage assembled on the reviewing stand across the way. They were all very young people, some of whom they'd already seen standing around by themselves. The girls and boys had lost their earlier allures and seemed perfectly natural, and not just by virtue of their costumes, dark ones. The way they were now, and the way they behaved with each other, was the way they were in reality. Up on the platform they weren't playing roles, didn't need to pose. They were all noble damsels or noble gentlemen by birth, or whatever the names were for such folk. And it wasn't their robes, diadems, or fans that did it, but the way they took their places and let themselves be looked at.

This effortless nobility communicated itself to the audience. It was the festival queen above all who, without lifting a finger, united the individuals on the street into a people. That came from the kind of beauty displayed by this young woman, who outside of the festival was probably just an adolescent, almost a child still. Nothing about her way of being beautiful was provocative or exciting. Or if it was exciting, then in the sense of getting things moving, of stirring up memories of something undefined, unclear, which became clear only now, in this moment. A beauty streamed from this queen-girl that touched everyone watching down below, as if this child were a close relative, the closest.

And then someone in the audience actually identified himself as such a relative. While the musicians began to play their trumpets and clarinets at the feet of the royal entourage, the driver heard a completely unfamiliar voice ring out right next to him, shouting an incomprehensible name. It was the poet shouting—the name of his daughter? Whom he was seeing for the first time? And he bawled in her direction that he was her father, almost screeching: "I've come, it's me, your father." And to the people who turned to look, "Yes, I'm her father!"

The queen turned toward him without losing her air of being-there-for-everyone. For a moment she showed joy, very briefly, yet in such a way that if this joy had had time to spread across her entire face, it would have been the most beautiful part of the festival.

"But that didn't happen," the pharmacist told me. "All of a sudden the girl became ugly. It was shock that did it. While she was apparently still looking at her father, in truth it was something in the back. I must describe this briefly: In the background a couple of policemen had just appeared. And then they arrested the little queen, in front of everyone. As they led her away, she looked back over her shoulder, seeking out her father. He promptly dropped everything and ran after her, accompanied by the athlete. After the poet and his friend had shown their identification, all three of them drove off in the police car. I stayed sitting there alone, motionless."

"And then? What then?" I asked. "Wasn't the girl's mother also nearby, the poet's former lover?"

"No."

"Had she died?"

"In my story no one dies," the pharmacist of Taxham replied. "Sometimes sad things happen, occasionally almost desperate things. But a death is out of the question."

"So: what was going on with her?"

"Have you forgotten? Leave it vague. Let's leave the business with the queen's mother vague. — Though I won't leave vague my reason for remaining seated, motionless, as the girl was taken away. You see, one time I witnessed just such a scene with my son. The gendarmes came to the house and took him away, with his hands twisted behind his back. And he looked back at me just like the poet's daughter. To this day I don't know why she was arrested. But my son was a thief. I mean, the first time he was arrested, he'd just been copying the little thefts his schoolmates pulled off for fun. He wasn't exactly an outsider, but in his age group he was always the last one to experience the things that solidified their group identity, and did so clearly without conviction or pleasure—just to be included. They phoned me to come and get him from the police station. For the moment he received only a warning, and was supposed to attend a few 'reeducation sessions' at the youth services agency. Out on the street in front of the police station I took my son in my arms. When I'd tried that at other times, I'd always felt him stiffen. This time he didn't. And we both cried. But then I hit him, hard, in the face. I can't explain it, except perhaps that of all illegal acts the one that always disgusted me the most was stealing. I even despise the gestures that go along with it—the sticky fingers, things being tucked into a pocket or jacket. And the facial expressions and twitches of a thief, even just an occasional thief, as he does his deed—a professional thief probably doesn't move a muscle—also disgust me, as if I were witnessing the most unnatural act imaginable. On the other hand, my sense of solidarity with my son had never been as strong as during those few minutes in front of the police station. One time, later, after his departure and disappearance, I even committed a theft myself, just a tiny little one—pilfering a pack of chewing gum, or a pencil. Still! Yet that didn't bring him back to me, either."

In retrospect it seemed to him he'd spent the rest of that night sitting there, and the following days and nights of the festival, too, and was still sitting there as he was here, telling me his story. For something else came up: In one of the musicians strolling from table to table that night he recognized his son.

Despite the arrest of the queen, the festival had to go on, and it helped that after the first few moments of consternation the music struck up. (In the brief interval, however, between the banging shut of the police car's last door and the trumpet's first note, the people out there had shown themselves united as neither before nor after—precisely in reaction to the shared shock: not one who didn't try to catch someone else's eye.)

It was a large instrumental group, without singers, mostly gypsies, who all seemed to come from the same family or tribe. But even the few non-gypsies, white-skinned and blond, were visibly, and then audibly, part of the family. They were playing almost exclusively wind instruments, rather small, stumpy ones, the trumpets short like the clarinets. And thus the music blared in a mighty yet short-winded racket, which for several measures at a time resembled a kind of stuttering in unison—unabashed, self-confident, and hymnic. Hymnic stuttering? Yes.

The only other kind of instrument was an accordion, always eye-catching when it was drawn apart, but clearly audible only occasionally, when it played a solo, fragments of a strangely soulful melody, in contrast to the rhythmic passages of the trumpets and clarinets. This accordion's keyboard was worked by his son. And among the few outsiders in the group, he was the one who could most easily have belonged to the tribe.

"It was not only because of prejudice," the pharmacist of Taxham said, "that for a long time I felt uneasy around gypsies. Probably unnecessary to mention that in my youth I even felt drawn to them, or to the hearsay about them. But later, in my travel and journeyman years, I was ambushed and robbed several times, and almost every time by gypsies. I'd told my son about this, too, and that the sight of this people, even from a distance, and even if it was small children or infants, fills me not with hatred but with panic: I promptly feel the knife held to my stomach again, all those hands under my shirt, even poking into my armpits."

And now he found his son among these gypsies, not only dressed like them but also with the same facial expression; he didn't know what to call it—neither "impudent" nor "shifty," perhaps closest to "there yet not there," unapproachable.

And so the son also gazed at his father while playing, almost kindly, but without focusing on him in particular, and just as kindly as all the other members of the orchestra, whose trumpets, always pointing slightly up into the night, gave off a much more powerful gleam than his modest accordion.

And the father was incapable of even making a sign to him. And he remained so throughout the rest of the days and nights of the festival. The musicians went on to the next table, made the rounds of the street, and filed past him again at the next sunrise or sunset, their trumpets glowing differently each time, the son unvaryingly kind, without any trace of tiredness, with his accordion. And something else came into play, on the very first night of the festival. The woman from the watershed fountain, the widow, the so-called winner, for him more the blow-striker and stone-hurler, turned up at the long table, was suddenly there, out of the darkness. His impulse was to recoil from her, step back a few paces, not out of fear but out of surprise, but he couldn't budge. And she did nothing but walk around him for a long time, her face always just a hand's breadth from his, silent, with wide eyes that seemed to want him gone.

Then at some point he managed to greet her and smile at her. But she didn't respond, merely circled the man once more and disappeared, with a last glance over her shoulder, like the earlier times.

Did he sleep at all during the festival? His memory says no. He stayed awake for several nights and days—which he'd always dreamed of, as something to experience, or as a possible turning point. And on the other hand he had a visual memory of waking up in an inn—the street also had a *posada*, right next to the church—and for a moment, just one, lying in his extremely narrow bed, with her back to him, is the strange woman.

And what's certain is that very soon the poet and the Olympic hero returned to the festival, with the festival queen between them, released now, and that for a long time afterward they were all just as mute as he was. (Only then did the poet finally notice that all this time the chauffeur hadn't spoken a single word.)

"Despite everything," the pharmacist of Taxham told me, "even despite my son, who soon vanished from my sight again—the last time I saw him, he was dancing with the young festival queen—I wasn't unhappy in the least, didn't wish for a second to be somewhere else. That's how it is! I thought. What mattered was to be out there in the nocturnal wind, with the others, with these particular people, for a while, and then to see what would happen next."

THREE

The person who told me this story stayed in that country long after the festival there. During this time he let two of his employees, mother and son, run the business in Taxham; these refugees from the civil war knew all about the various medications, those for physical ills and more particularly those for what went beyond; and when it came to dosages, they also knew the right proportions; and besides, in the presence of these two and what they had so obviously gone through, some customers were promptly cured of what ailed them.

For the time being he stayed on at the inn in the lower town. The street, as became apparent with the first light of day, led directly to a sandy and rocky steppe, which apparently wasn't cultivated. Seen from the window of his inn, this steppe looked not completely flat but hilly in places, alternating perfectly level surfaces with gently rising ones, and extending into the vast and empty distance, to all the horizons except the one at his back, which was blocked by the random clusters of houses, large and small, in the lower town and the stern line of the upper town stretched far along its cliff. The entire town, surrounded by wasteland as far as the eye could see, seemed sealed off from the rest of the continent, the latter hardly accessible.

Yet trains still traversed the steppe twice a day, or at least at the time when this story takes place, or did the tooting perhaps come from a tractor trailer instead? And even though there was no airport, all day long the sky remained populated, and not only by birds: A flight path must have crossed the area, not a heavily used one, to be sure—only two or three jet trails per day—but at least they suggested you weren't completely cut off from the rest of the world. These jet trails were always very high up, or rather deep up, deep into the consistently blue sky, or even beyond it, and when the plane belonging to a trail actually came into view for a change, with a momentary flash, or for a second could even be heard—a delicate hum in the remotest part of the atmosphere—those who found themselves beneath it received the unmistakable impression that the plane already had thousands of such flight miles behind it, had taken off long ago in an entirely different country, and would remain out there for a long time at the same altitude.

. . .

The inn also served as the bar for the steppe street, and was managed by the young girl, the queen for the few days of the festival. Her mother, the actual owner, remained absent during the entire time, and my storyteller also told me that if one reader or another really needed some sort of explanation I could add that maybe she had set out to find her former lover and surprise him, and was just then roaming around his part of the world, as the poet was roaming around hers; they'd just missed each other.

The girl, left alone in charge, was having a hard time of it. Of course, the place must have been run-down even before this. Much was broken or unusable, and seemed to have been that way a long time, and many things were missing—had disappeared? or had never been there at all? The sink in one of the rooms had no drain, while the one in another room let the water flow out directly onto the floor. Not one bed was long enough (except perhaps for the dwarfs in the area, of whom there were quite a few—had the inn originally been intended for them?). And the rooms themselves were so small that instead of walking, at most you could take one step at a time: one step from the door to the bed, likewise one step from the door to the window, and from the bed to the window, the bed to the wash basin; and from the wash basin to the view out the window not even one step was possible—or necessary?

For as the days passed, he came to accept such cramped space for living and sleeping, and then to like it; if he slept at all, he slept deeply there, quietly and dreamlessly—unusual for him; and when he sat there, especially in the morning—there was hardly anything else you could do in these rooms—he sat so still, with a few everyday objects within reach, that from time to time just sitting there felt like a form of activity, perhaps even one that was good for something.

What wasn't good, however, was the lack of keys to the doors, even to the inn's entrance downstairs, or of bolts on the inside. He wanted to be able to lock himself in there, at least now and then, but even in the lavatory that wasn't possible. Some of the windowpanes were also broken. The threshold at the front door, as high as a person's shinbone, was rotted and partially caved in. The roof wasn't exactly missing, but here and there the tiles had been tossed or pushed on top of each other, not by a nocturnal wind but by a storm. And the gutter was clogged with steppe debris that had accumulated there, was gummed up with the sand that had also blown in from there, sand that not even the copious dew of the region could wash away. And the usual highland firewood, which elsewhere was stacked under the windows along the street, was strewn all over the back courtyard and also inside the inn's kitchen.

Yet the building and its major and minor features exuded an aura of nobility: the stone walls with their bluish granite shimmer; the interior walls, not smooth anywhere, and slightly bulging and wavy, clad up to eye level with small tiles; next to a plastic cup, a blackened silver spoon; a stuffed wolf and, in a dark corner of the inn, a tall, slim cast-iron stove, where even now, in midsummer, a wood fire burned constantly, visible behind the old-time translucent, flameproof stove door made of mica, the firelight transmitted by the sheet of mica to the wolf's glass eyes; a football game table—most of its figurines missing their heads or legs—and in the glass case next to it a Moorish wedding robe; in the inn's bathroom, the only larger space besides the bar, the doorknob, the tub feet, the towel racks made of rock crystal, and the door of pressboard, and the tub itself of the kind of metal used for cans, and on the rock crystal towel racks, a whole batch of them poking in star form out of the tiled wall, one small washcloth, which even when wet was stiff as a board.

During the street festival the three of them remained busy with other things. One time, long after midnight, a herd of bulls was driven through the streets, coming from the steppe, very young ones, not yet trained for fighting, but with horns that were already almost full-grown, and anyone who felt like it could run ahead of them; at least no one stayed in his seat. (Or did someone?) And one time, on the eighth and final day of the festival, which was called *verbena*, a silent procession passed by, with statues of saints carried in front, and canopies, under one of them the hunters who lived on the street, under another the chess players who lived there, under the third the Holy of Holies; the procession circled far out onto the steppe, so far that the squawking of jackdaws and magpies was replaced by that of eagles and buzzards, and upon their return to the city, not one marcher's Sunday best wasn't covered with dust up to the knees and stuck everywhere with thistle thorns.

And one day an eclipse of the sun was part of the street festival; the first moment of it, the first tiny slicing of the moon's orb across that of the sun was rather like a bite being taken out of the sun, and long after the end of the festival this image continued to burn and glow on many people's retinas, a sort of photographic negative.

But then it was time to give the girl a hand with the inn (she continued to display some of her queenliness there). Besides, not a few parts of that street on the edge of the steppe, where the Ascension feast tables had stood just a little while ago, now reverted to the work sites they had been earlier. In place of the reviewing stand for the royal entourage, the disappearing underground of the sewer workers, and at the main gathering place for the musicians—when they hadn't been strolling up and down the street—the resumption of the paving operation, heading toward the steppe, and from the wide-open church, being freshly whitewashed, instead of the sound of the organ, voices from the painters' transistor radios. Especially when the workers had gone to get something to eat and their tools were standing or lying around unused, it was tempting to pick up a shovel, hammer, hose, or tool chest and go to work with it.

And in fact the three of them did go to work in this fashion. One of the pavers, while leveling the asphalt, playfully tossed them a wire brush; it landed at their feet, and one of the three bent down and began to scrape away at the exterior walls of the inn, at first also just in play or trying it out, but then without stopping, intently, and continued working this way and in other ways, and elsewhere, on the building for an entire week. And similarly one of the three picked up an orphaned carpenter's level on the street, and so on.

In the inn—in a glass case, along with top hats and officers' caps—were also the work clothes common in that region, which were then handed out to them by the barmaid, and one of them worked in a blue tunic, the other in a white one. And after just a few days they could hardly be distinguished from the more or less professional workers on the street. Their hair now almost impossible to get a comb through. Dragging footsteps. Sagging pants seats. Loud, thoughtless talking, such as you hear from roofers, for instance—actually a necessity when one of them has to communicate from up on the ridgepole with another down on the ground.

And so they periodically went with the other crews to get a drink of water at the only public fountain on this slightly sloping street, just a pipe poking out of a wall, from which a trickle of spring water ran constantly; and during the noon hour they lay under the only tree on the entire street, and on its only patch of grass, sprawled among the painters and pavers—but who was who?—without anyone's saying a word.

The only one who didn't get completely caught up in his task, even though he did manual work like the others, who seemed disguised somehow, was the poet. Without his being sloppy or clumsy, or shirking work—on the contrary: he immediately did whatever he was told—whatever he did had a slight casualness to it, and even after the greatest exertion he didn't pause to catch his breath with the others but promptly went off somewhere, out of the circle or the triangle. And so the local workers soon sensed that in reality he wasn't really a threshold-repairer and window-shutter-painter at all; no, it was more like a suspicion. "You're not what you say you are, and not anything worthwhile, either." And not until he presented himself mainly as a chef, at first just for his daughter, later, as the offerer of little delicacies to those resting out by the fountain, did he become a believable worker: That was how jolly the atmosphere became all around him, how caught up he seemed in the hacking of bones or the most meticulous dredging in flour or the plucking of down, how flushed he grew even over a cold stove.

When it came to all the different sorts of repairs that had to be done on the old inn, the former star athlete, the forgotten Olympic medalist and world champion, turned out to be quite amazing. It was understandable that from his period of fame and his short-lived wealth he knew his way around hotels, pensions, and bars—he'd owned several such properties, though at increasingly short intervals he'd become known as the "owner on the run." But who would have thought that the world champion in downhill skiing would get such pleasure out of patching, clearing out, tidying, cleaning, sanding down dining-room tables, and all for others, for strangers? In addition to the more strenuous tasks, for which he was the one among the three who was the planner, assigner, and supplier of materials, and without showing off at all, he was filled with enthusiasm for those kinds of activities known as "services." During the time there in the *posada* he made the others' beds, shined their shoes, ironed everything in sight that needed ironing, did the shopping, sewed and darned, and always promptly and with few words. If he was no longer a champion or a businessman, he was something like a cheerful caretaker, at least around the inn. His face glowed when he brought a glass to someone's table. And you could easily picture him in his youth on the gold-medal podium.

Altogether, it was only in this way that the old athlete acquired a face. And what was it like? It made it possible for you to call him by name, again for the first time, the given name that could finally be spoken out loud: "Hey, Alfons!; Hey, Alfonso!" To which he merely said, "Yes, a person's got to work. This work is my vacation, my leisure. I've never had so much leisure time. A person's got to work."

Except that in the midst of his élan this face time and again, for a brief frozen instant, seemed stricken with hopelessness: "No, I'm done for. There's no hope for me."

Meanwhile, from the inn's front door, the pavers could be seen behind their fire, distorted by the flames and the smoke: "If only I could at least stand in a fire like that!"

It was chiefly this shared work that made the storyteller stay with the two others. Once the repairs were done, he increasingly lost track of the athlete and the poet. One factor was that the latter moved out of the inn, closer to town, to the center of Santa Fe (soon followed, as always, by his companion). His daughter had disappeared in the meantime—following the festival musicians, people said. Yes, the festival could still be smelled along the entire length of the street, precisely in its absence.

And without a word, he, the storyteller, had allowed the accordion player, his son—if indeed it was him—to move on. "It was the right thing to do," he said. "Father and child have to go their separate ways eventually. And this time it was the moment, and maybe not a bad one. Right? At any rate, suddenly I was the only person living in that inn there on the edge of the savanna."

Here his search began for the woman known as the "winner." Yet shouldn't he have been afraid of her? The wounds she'd inflicted on him with her bare hands during that first night of struggle—a one-sided struggle—still weren't completely healed. Especially the one on his forehead, on the spot where he'd had the small growth removed earlier, kept starting to bleed again, seemingly for no reason. And that was exactly where the blow out of nowhere had struck him way back then on the end of the woods by the Salzburg airport—"way back then?" yes, that was his thought.

But he wanted to and had to find the woman, even if it might involve a third blow on the head. This was the first time he'd been fired up with passion this way, "and perhaps less for the object of it," he said, "than for the trailing and tracking down." A piece of the woman's fingernail, broken off during her violent act and picked up from the floor by him in that mountain house, had seemed to him a clue rather than a bad omen. Looking at it, he felt all the more intensely that she must be nearby.

Yet she no longer made herself noticeable. Once, on the edge of the steppe, when something struck him hard on the

head, it was an apple, but where was the tree?—none there—
but where was the thrower?—none far and wide—and only
then did he see, already at some distance, the raven from
whose beak the fruit had presumably fallen, out of the clear
blue sky.

To an outsider, his searching was barely noticeable. Simply by
staying in his blue work clothes, so practical and good-looking,
he managed not to stand out at all in that town on the steppe,
which wasn't large, merely spread out. And likewise his movements, facial expressions, glances were more like those of
someone hurrying from one workplace to another; no looking
to the side, no pausing. But in his mind, too, he often wasn't
paying attention to what he was doing: "Precisely because she
seemed overwhelmingly powerful to me, she could go out of
my mind between one step and the next. The search for the
woman felt so significant and urgent that there were times
when my consciousness couldn't keep a grip on it anymore,
when I literally forgot about it for long stretches and was
thinking of something entirely different, which, however, had
the same glowing intensity as what I was supposed to track
down—the way you're sometimes so filled with gratitude that
you forget to say thank you."

For days and days he roamed through Santa Fe, mostly
through the lower town, where the weather from the surrounding savanna was much more extreme and said to him,
"Hot!"

Only a couple of times did he follow the alley up to the old quarter on top of the cliff, still a center, but as a rule he did that only toward evening, when the squares up there, in contrast to those down below, gradually emptied out and the nocturnal wind then made its presence felt, with a force very different from down in the lower town. To stand in the uppermost and most deserted of the squares, on the edge of the cliff, and let his face, the roots of his hair, his memory, and who knows what else be refreshed by this wind, blowing out of the blackness. "I'm a nocturnal-wind person. And where are my nocturnal-wind people?" Responding not with his palate or tongue, but with his temples.

And in such a nocturnal wind he also found himself thinking one time that he was glad to have been struck dumb. Good that he couldn't speak any longer. He'd never have to open his mouth again. Freedom! Even more: the ideal condition! Establish a party, even a religion: the party of the mute, the religion of muteness? No, remain alone with it. Mute, free, and ultimately, as it should be, alone.

In another nocturnal-wind moment he again received a blow on the head, or at least he felt as if he did; in reality he was merely brushed by the coat of a mouse, spat out by an owl, sitting on a wall somewhere, that had just choked down its prey.

In the daytime he invariably stayed down at the foot of the cliff. "Foot of the cliff" didn't mean, however, that from there the town extended right onto the plain. Beyond the two rivers that came together here, the terrain immediately rose again, only much flatter, then fell off, and so on, till it reached the rocky steppe.

The many cliffs, as well as the crevasses, and gorges (with rivers and brooks) created unusual echo conditions throughout the town. These conditions didn't merely amplify sounds. They also confused your sense of direction, even where up and down were concerned. Near and far also often became indistinguishable. Especially in the morning, when far and wide only a few people were up—sleeping late seemed to be the habit in this region—suddenly two voices would be talking loudly right under his window at the inn, and when he leaned out to look, no one was there, not a soul on the street; but way out on the steppe he could just make out two gesticulating figures, no bigger than dots, yet every word echoing clearly in his tiny room.

Or during the deepest, most silent night, nothing but the monotonous hooting of the owls—from down below? from up above?—and from one of the river narrows, the one in which the only larger gardens on the savanna were laid out, following the course of the rather sporadic flow of water, came the small sound of a watchdog gulping for air, one of several, the sound promptly echoed by the cliffs and now answered by the dog with its first bark, which, along with the echo, the next dog promptly returned, which in turn was followed by that bark's echo, doubled by the narrowing of the valley, whereupon a third dog up the valley chimed in, along with its echo, multiplied by a curve in the river, and all this getting louder and louder, the echo being multiplied through the entire highland and lowland, until in the end—no, no end for a long time, it seems—although it's only three dogs there barking at each other, it's as if a whole army of dogs were launching an all-out attack.

It was still summer, yet you could become completely confused as to the time of year. That had little to do with the numerous electronic thermometers in the town, each of which displayed a different temperature, often with variations almost as large as those between summer and winter. The leaf drop, sometimes even in early July, wasn't altogether unusual, either.

No, here there was a curious back and forth between the seasons, one minute way ahead, the following just as far back. On one of the days there the storyteller went for a swim in the river, the one that had more water, with the whispering or rustling of the poplars on both banks and that summery sound of crickets chirping, if there ever was one, and all of a sudden—he was swimming upstream—a seemingly unending deluge of fallen leaves swept toward him, yellow, red, blackish, an interminable train, drifting on and under the water in garlands, which further reinforced the autumnal impression—while in the next moment a cuckoo could be heard, as if it were at most late spring.

And that mulberry tree that still had almost all its fruit, most of it unripe, while the one in Taxham had long since dropped all its berries, and even the red stains on the ground had long since faded. And likewise the elderberry here, blooming in cream-colored dots, while in that same instant your eye lit on the sunflower fields, blackened as in November

and reminiscent of world-war cemeteries, above which, however, midsummery air still shimmered.

Yet he hardly lost his way, and when he did, he calmly let it
happen; now, right now was the moment to experience something like this.

Many of the local folk lost their way more often than he
did. Again and again he, the person most a stranger to the
place, would be asked for directions, and usually he could help,
too, with a mute gesture.

True: those who asked him were sometimes tourists, but
just from the province whose capital the nocturnal-wind town
was, people from the country; there weren't any other tourists.
And these tourists or day-trippers were a welcome sight, in
their inconspicuous outfits, and especially with their timidity
in this unfamiliar territory, and also with their little exuber-
ances, such that even old folks could be seen skipping (just one
step each time).

Once he saw a wedding procession tearing along the main
street in the lower town in cars decorated with streamers,
accompanied by rather cautious honking, clanging of tin cans,
and then he caught sight, in the newlyweds' car, of two such
oldsters, obviously from a village.

But as a rule, when he was out walking, searching for the
woman or with his thoughts elsewhere, he kept his eyes on
the ground. As he wandered out of the town onto the

all-encompassing steppe, he thus regularly came upon a few mushrooms, various kinds that were familiar to him, even if they were varieties specific to the region, deviating from the general species.

These he then ate, sometimes even on the street, or in a bar, always the same one, because there he needed only one or two gestures to make himself understood. It was striking how strange, even uncanny these things that grew in their own region were to the natives. When it came to the most common and most tasty mushroom—to be found wherever you went, even behind the houses—they viewed him as someone gambling with his life, and they almost backed away, as if the very sight were life-threatening, yet some—many—seemed attracted by the mushrooms, more as a marvel than the devil's handiwork.

But many other plants or fruits from their own region were also unfamiliar or taboo to the inhabitants, and not only those in the town. One day he came to a settlement on the outskirts similar to the street with the inn, with the same squat, longish buildings, extending up the slopes of the steppe, but on another side of town, and there he picked in passing a fig from a tree growing right next to a doorway, whereupon an old woman ran out, shouting—not because he was stealing, but because of the presumably poisonous type of fig: "Don't eat that!" In her entire life she'd never tasted the figs, and now she wanted to preserve him from being done in by her doorway figs.

Beneath her troubled gaze he then ate precisely two of the fruits, which tasted so delicious he would have liked to eat every one on the tree, but took only the smallest. This ignorance on the part of even the oldest inhabitants about what was growing right by their door, along with their fear of it, was something he encountered from morning till night.

A couple of times during this period of searching he also ran into his two traveling companions. Although they'd separated only temporarily, the poet and the star athlete acted as though they no longer knew their driver. Or perhaps when they saw him out on the street, far from the car and the inn, they actually didn't recognize him, a phenomenon he was used to from Taxham.

And they also overlooked him because they seemed to be preoccupied with something else entirely. They, too, were searching, but much more obviously than he was. What were they looking for? A fight? Money? An audience? A helper, more effective than he was, one who would save them, not just for one evening but once and for all? And not a lone savior, but a whole savior people, a people of saviors? Or weren't they looking instead for one who would destroy them at last—their terminator, their executioner? And each time the two of them appeared more ragged, in spite of the elegant suits with which they'd replaced their work clothes. Finally they even turned up almost completely toothless, and that in the space of just a few days. Or had they had false teeth before, which they'd now lost or swallowed?

Sometimes their faces were beet red, sometimes pale as death. The loose soles of their shoes flapped as they walked. There were sticky trails—like those of snails—across their beards. The only part of them that still seemed neat and proper was their carefully manicured fingernails (which additionally gave them the air of deviant killers).

Thus they roamed, probably ceaselessly, almost day and night, making grandiose gestures, through the upper and lower town, blocking the path of other pedestrians, making fun of them for their appearance, their gait, their voices, but it was like a game, and their invective was rhymed, in poetic form, and sometimes also sung, with the result that no one stopped them, and they were even paid now and then for their performances.

One time he saw them on the Plaza Mayor in the upper town, on the hottest day of the year, offering blocks of ice for sale, "not artificially frozen, or fallen off a truck, but born during the Ice Age in primeval muck, then by Emperor Constantine as imperial ice chosen." And another time they blocked his way down on the large bridge over the river, again without recognizing him, and wanted him to take their picture (which he did), their faces garishly painted, jet-black raven and magpie feathers in their hair.

He walked past all the town's pharmacies—and there were unusually many of them for a provincial town like this, almost two dozen; he didn't need anything, after all, wasn't sick; or was there something he could take to get his voice back?

He saw hardly any old pharmacists there, and also hardly any old interiors. All these highland pharmacists made a robust impression, and had rough-skinned faces and hands, as if in their free time or in general they were mountain climbers or hikers, or at any rate more at home out of doors than here, with the cosmetics in Aisle 1 and the medicine case in Aisle 2.

He saw the only old pharmacist in the upper town, in the only pharmacy up there, it, too, new or renovated: Once, when this man had night duty, his face appeared in the little hatch next to the locked door, yet with no customer anywhere in sight on the nocturnal-wind street—perhaps he wanted a breath of air; and once in the middle of the day as a silhouette against the large rear window that looked out directly over the cliff's sheer drop, a cliff window, through which the profile of the old man, alone in the place, without employees, stood out against the steppe, devoid of people as far into the distance as the eye could see—grass-, sand-, and cliff-yellow, now bleached almost white in the midday sun, and out there on the street he felt as if he were seeing his self-portrait, from later on.

The only person with whom my storyteller had contact now was the proprietor of an out-of-the-way bar in the lower town. (But what does "out-of-the-way" mean? Every other one of the many bars seemed like that, and also bore such a name: "Hideaway" or "Corner.") This bartender was also old, in such a way that everything about him, instead of turning wrinkled and white, had become callused and bristly. Without his having to open his mouth it was clear the man was a widower, had been one for a long time, and his children had gone away even longer ago, never to be seen again, and this was the last season that he would spend behind the bar and that this place would exist at all. And he wouldn't be around to see the next year arrive.

"Whenever I came into the place, the proprietor would be standing not behind his bar but in the middle of the tiled room, which you entered by going down a few steps, in dim fluorescent light. And not until he recognized me as a guest would he duck down and slip under the bar flap into his realm. And he didn't open his mouth any more than I did. In any case, he had only one beverage to offer, which filled his shelves from top to bottom in identical bottles. Only what he placed before me in the way of snacks varied. But there was no need to ask for these in any case—the olives, the pistachios, the miniature octopuses that he deep-fried in a flash, the partridge eggs, the crayfish, the mushrooms— which I brought and he prepared in silence; what he served was entirely up to him! So we stood, with the bar between us, always just the two of us, and as a rule looked past one another, while he used my presence as a pretext for eating and drinking like me, the same things and in the same rhythm. His hair stuck straight up, motionless and stiff, way above his head, and also stuck out of his ears and nostrils. The counter was a thick slab of white marble, part of which formed a shallow basin, where there was always some water, perfectly clear, without a drain: In this hollow he would wash the glasses, dull with age, after every use, each one separately, after scooping out the water and pouring in fresh. And things were at their most silent in the *rincón* when all the small, delicate glasses had been washed and placed in rows on the marble, and the hollow had been filled with fresh water again, everything else had been put away, neither of us was eating or drinking anymore, and instead we were both gazing at the neatly lined-up old shot glasses and the bit of water, so clear, in the drainless hollow, this round miniature pool with its bright marble bottom, just as, perhaps at that very moment, in a temple garden in faraway Asia, a visitor and a monk might be sitting on a boulder in the middle of an empty patch of sand, raked in long, wavy rows to represent the Sea of Japan."

One morning my storyteller came upon another settlement on the outskirts, the kind that could be found all around, extending into small dead-end gorges and climbing the rocky slopes of the steppe to left and right. And again the general smallness of the houses, actually stone huts: wherever rock walls protruded between them and behind them, even the lowest were taller than the dwellings.

Only one of the roads leading into the settlement continued all the way to the top; the rest soon gave way to steep steps.

At the various levels, here and there, and easy to pick out among the small structures, stood a few cars, not many, and it seemed more as if they were enthroned one above the other on the slope, with one car, as high and as long as a house, way at the top, already beyond the edge of town, on a promontory, as the lead or chief vehicle.

When my storyteller now broke into a run, quite out of character, and only for a few steps, he knew what he was doing. Most of the huts lower down had benches out in front, facing the sunrise, and when they weren't occupied, which was the exception, the electric meters on the exterior walls, enclosed in glass boxes, revealed the presence of residents, actually residents who didn't merely lodge there but rather were keeping mighty busy inside: Almost all the little counters were turning quite fast, some even speeding and racing.

But the higher he climbed in the settlement, the slower the counters turned. Where initially all he had seen was the even flashing of the metal disk as it spun around, up here even the painted markings could be made out. In the glass boxes higher up the slope, some little disks were motionless. And this motionlessness increased steadily as he went up. Also most of these houses had their shutters rolled down, and hardly a chimney had smoke coming out.

How strange, this motionlessness of the metal disks in the morning sun. Yet even up here, among the rocks, more and more of them, there were still outdoor lights, even some on poles that were quite shiny and new and stuck up above the houses, and fat electrical cables, several bunched together, strung every which way, the most insignificant structure more than amply serviced. At the same time, most of the houses didn't look neglected at all, even if they were abandoned, for the day, or longer. One, located almost at the top where the settlement ended, had a for-sale sign and was ready for immediate occupancy. To one side of it, above the flat line of its roof, children out playing were just climbing, in single file, up the hilly steppe, already completely deserted there, their silhouettes visible against the early sky. Like the tall savanna grass on the ridge, their hair had a brightly shining streak on top, lighter than straw.

"If the house had had a view of the steppe, I would have been a buyer that very day. But of course all the windows faced the town on the cliff." And after a bend in the road, he came upon the first ruins. Here there were suddenly not only no more electric meter boxes, but also no doors and roofs. Small trees had rooted in the crumbled squares, almost always figs; at their feet, in the rubble, mattresses and bottomless pots and pans. But nearby there could still be a bit of a vegetable garden, blooming or bearing well despite the steep ground, or an overgrown chicken pen.

And only after that, the last of the last in the settlement, even higher up on the steppe, came a structure that couldn't be meant for domestic animals or raising plants, or even for storing garden tools. It was a sort of shack, a fairly large one, even cantilevered somewhat over the ledge on which it was situated. Despite its size, it gave the impression of having no interior space, more a frame than a shack; as if there were no room left for either tools or animals, and certainly not for a human being. True, there was a door, made of wood, like the rest of the building, wood that had apparently been gathered from far and wide, even several doors. But these stood, no, leaned, one against the other, and if you pushed or lifted one out of the way—that was the only possibility for opening them—you would immediately come upon the next one, and so on, until instead of reaching a room you would find yourself out in the open again.

And it was similar with the so-called walls: as if they were nothing more than stacks of lumber, piled and staggered one close to the other all the way to the back, for instance parts salvaged from the house ruins farther down, also old window frames as material, not mounted to let in air and light, however, but propped at an angle or laid flat, stuffed with beams and boards, and all this stuff every which way, such that the only space you could imagine inside would accommodate no more than a rat- or mousehole.

Simply incomprehensible, this structure at the very top of the cliffs. What is it? What's it meant for? What it resembles most is a barricade. Except that on top of this barricade—the only part with any shape to it, the only recognizable shape in this heap of boards and planks—is a railing, a sort of balustrade or gallery. A barricade with a lookout platform? But otherwise nothing: no stovepipe, no tarpaulins, not a single head of lettuce.

And this is already quite far past the last streetlights and electric lines, and yet the passable street extends most of the way here, and not far from the apparent barricade is parked that house-long automobile, almost a bus, another Santana jeep, though considerably larger than the one that passed them on the trip here, and this one has its headlights protected from the stones of the steppe by little grilles.

Past the empty car and scrambling up the protruding pieces of wood—no ladder anywhere to be seen—to the railing. ("First, though, I took a few steps back," he told me. "How the world begins to move with your stepping back that way, as it does with going forward only occasionally in childhood!") And from the balustrade there becomes visible, down below in the shack or framework, reachable by way of an interior ladder, something like a space or a shell after all. Not climbing down into it, merely lying up there on his stomach, looking down for a long time. A bed, or rather a makeshift sleeping place, squeezed in below amidst all the wood. And a blanket, too, thrown off just this morning; otherwise nothing, nothing at all, the most extreme contrast to the triumphant splendor in the watershed house; and at that moment, no one to be seen.

"Is that how she was mourning her husband?" I asked. "Or trying to do penance for something?"

No answer from my storyteller, or then this: "During my travels, I was often lonely—something I could never say of myself otherwise. One time I took a piece of bread from the counter in a bar and carried it around with me for a while because it smelled of the perfume of the woman who had probably sliced it. Or on the street I looked for drunks, just to be jostled by them a bit as I passed. And I would push or pull open the same shop doors as the stranger in front of me. And in the bathroom at the inn I dried myself not with the clean towel but with the used one the person before me had left in a corner. And in public places, for sugar for my coffee, I always took the lumps that had already been unwrapped and had a piece broken off. But the loneliness there in the shack! (No, it was really more an inhabited barricade.) The 'winner'! From reading medieval epics I know that such epithets or names often signify the opposite. So from the outset the 'winner' is a 'loser.' Of course, the secret of the epics is that if the adventure turns out well for a change, the 'loser' then actually becomes a 'winner'—if ever there was one. She was given that name so that, or because, she could—or should—become one in reality. To become a winner was the destiny of the current

loser. And somewhere in between, the adventure would perhaps take place."

He leaped down from the shack. Wind sprang up. There
was something that had to be done! From now on he had to
keep focused on the task, or, as he, the smell-man, put it, "nose
to track." And stick to it—for what? To discover something, or
rediscover something.

That same day he encountered the poet and the star athlete for
the last time in his story.

That town of Santa Fe, at least its larger lower section, was
as loud as any normal town. But he'd never heard screaming
there, not of the kind he heard now. Children, soccer fans,
crane-guiders, lottery-ticket vendors, criers of all sorts didn't
scream like this. It was approaching noon, and he was just
passing an abandoned bull-fighting arena in a rather out-of-
the-way place, an arena that wouldn't be used again until the
next year, for the annual *corrida* had already taken place in
early summer; the *feria* posters from June looked ancient. And
the screaming came from outside, from a no-man's-land spandrel between the street and the curve of the arena, on the
somewhat neglected side, with seats that most people tried to
avoid in summertime because they were directly in the sun;
though for the late fall motor-cross races and concerts had
been announced.

On this outside strip, strewn with shreds of plastic and
scraps of paper spiked on isolated thistles, his two companions
were standing with a young man. He was the one who was

screaming. Several other young people were there, keeping at a distance. During the last few weeks it had happened again and again that people had gone after each other out in the open, serious for a moment, then turning it in no time into a mock fight: That was common in this country. But here it was in earnest, as you could see from the way the boy was dancing back and forth in front of the two others, and hear in his screams, actually directed more to one side. Not once in his life had he screamed this way. Up to now all that had come from him, in passing on the street, for a decade, was at most a murmuring, incomprehensible, and sometimes spitting. But now the moment had come, and he screamed his battle cries at th top of his voice. "Kill! I'm going to kill both of you!" So at l the two had been recognized, though perhaps in a differ way from what they'd expected.

Figures like this boy had turned up more and more
late. Although each went around by himself, or at m
one other person, they'd come to form a real horde on
avenues, but also on paths through the steppe, cheek by jowl with each other, a horde in the face of which the rest of the region's population increasingly appeared as the minority.

Out in the open, these characters, who were sometimes not all that young, were coming more and more into the foreground. The central squares, the bridges, even the entrances to public buildings were black almost exclusively with them. They stared right through the other passersby and also didn't respond to either greetings or the simplest question. In each other's presence they also remained silent, or fell silent the moment someone who didn't belong to their group approached.

Thus it became evident that they did belong together after a fashion. It was as if they rejected ordinary language, and even acted as though they didn't understand it. They had a language all their own, and they wanted to keep it to themselves. Keeping it to themselves meant that in their region—and it was their very own region, for hadn't they obviously constituted the vast majority for a long while now?—no one and nothing should hold sway but them and their language, and, connected with that, their claim to land ownership and power in these parts, which they would seize without further ado, and as soon as possible. Their habit of staring into the air out in public suggested a secret understanding. And never the slightest flicker of an expression, even with new people joining them day after day, and certainly never a smile, meant either for the person next to or behind them, or for or about themselves.

By virtue of their numbers alone they seemed connected. Yet each one was poised for a collective, instantaneous, and unprecedentedly violent overthrow. One or the other would pose as a kind of challenger just by appearing on the street. Not that he would block the path of the others, who seemed to be growing increasingly scarce. It was mostly a certain way of walking, intended to provoke, a loose-kneed, almost boneless saunter, a glide, an ostentatious display of absentness, and then a sudden pounce, seemingly directed at someone, then just missing him, eyes staring into nowhere.

These challengers were so deformed that it was often impossible to make out whether they were men or women. What they resembled most closely, with their casual movements, was women who've aged prematurely and intentionally make themselves look even older, uglier, and more shapeless, an insult hurled in the face of the world—and who then suddenly, eye to eye with the other person, with a jerk, at the speed of lightning, stiffen to become a squad of killers.

And the poet, who couldn't refrain from getting involved whenever something excited him one way or the other, had now fallen into the trap of one of these challengers. It was entirely likely that he had taken the boy to task, without thinking twice, saying that the boy's intentions or ideas were unknown or of no interest to him, likely that the mere appearance and gait of the stranger coming toward him had irritated him to the point where he burst out cursing him in a language and with words that the object of his abuse did understand after all, in a flash and at one blow.

What became apparent: the poet was utterly incapable of defending himself. He couldn't use force, had never used force. As when in a dream you may want to hit someone, but the blows lose their strength just before they reach the other person's body and land at most as little taps, so he now experienced this in reality. It was still more remarkable that even the Olympic champion, adept in many sports, was unable to engage in even the smallest fight, and not because he happened to be drunk; he, too, had never defended himself, he, too, was defenseless, and had been so since childhood. And he was the one whose measure the assailant was now taking.

The youth had no knife. Yet he didn't need any weapon, as he was demonstrating on the athlete, in complete silence now, without screaming: The dizzying succession of blows he was miming would end with one that would prove deadly. The boy, who on closer inspection turned out to have a wrinkled, oldish face, was plainly working himself up for an execution as he repeated, faster and faster, the pantomime of blows and death blows aimed at the athlete, who stood there stiff as a board; but the execution was meant for the poet next to him, who had likewise frozen.

"I realized: My story was at risk," my storyteller said. "And I cared about my story—and how! But if I'd continued to stand by, it would've been done for, and everything that had gone before null and void. The same was true of turning my back, leaving the scene, looking away. And I didn't want my story to be taken from me. That couldn't happen! No!" It was the first word to cross his lips in a long time, almost inaudible, through clenched teeth. And then he said, in the same way, "Calm down, heart." And his heart calmed down. That could happen.

Nowhere in his entire life had he gone on the defensive; he'd been unable, or unwilling, to strike back. His only form of self-defense was calm; to become the epitome of calm. And now he simply ran down this fellow who, directly in front of his two victims, was chopping the air into smaller and smaller pieces, a hair's breadth from their heads and throats, warming up for two neck-breaking blows. He ran him down, and the man slumped against the wall of the arena and didn't get up. That, too, could happen.

And after that the bystanders let the three go away together without more ado, some of them even seeming to approve of what had taken place; as if in any case it hadn't been the moment for an act of violence that would unleash everything else, still too early for the outbreak of war in this country. And the driver's car was standing right around the corner. That, too, could happen. And only now came a trembling, affecting everyone but him. His calm persisted.

That he then sent them home, mute once more, with an imperious gesture—having pressed the car keys, his own, into the poet's hand and pointed them in the right direction—was like the slap he'd given his son that time he'd picked him up at the police station (he, the father, had been on the verge of striking out at the handcuff policeman).

The two pals obeyed. But first they all had a farewell drink in the bar at the inn. There the former Olympic champion suddenly began chanting—it was a real chanting—a singsong recitation: "The stench at home in the barn. Milk squirted into the manure by the mad cow. My mother dying from a kick in the chest by the horse. Sparks from the pellet stove flying across the screen in the village movie theater. Looking under teachers' skirts. Playing hopscotch among bomb craters. Stretching in bed and bumping into the stinging nettles Father had spread at the foot to dry. Our neighbor kicking his own son around outside the front door. Sleeping in a cornfield as a recruit. The sparks from the edges of my skis flying across the television screen. My brother vanished in Canada. My first love married to a Latter-Day Saint. The snow in Japan versus that in South America. My leg broken in the nighttime giant slalom. My father also dead for a long time now. My sister also dead for a long time now. The sparks from hundreds of horses' hooves flying over the cemetery. The locks on the apartment changed by my last love with her own hands. No longer making it by the skin of my teeth. The medal sold, and not just once. Letting myself go. But up to now still always finding my way home. And the sparks in the darkness flying across the screen. And sitting in the summer twilight with bats all around. And sitting on winter nights with friends. And as for 'home,' associating it neither with the place nor the house but with the wagon roads through the fields."

He shook the driver's hand, and the poet, fixing his eyes unblinkingly on the driver, again as if he knew at least something about him and his story, stood up and said, "They rode from morning to evening, always straight ahead. A steady stream of butterflies flew by and shooed away any second thoughts. A cricket sat at the entrance to her cave, a veritable Pythia. The solution couldn't come from purposeful pondering, but from an entirely different direction. Unlike in the days of kings, there was no higher authority. But why was there no higher authority? Never, at any time of year, had he been so alone. Ah, to write poetry the way mountain climbers talk with each other while dangling on the rope! Ah, born in Austria! But who could spend his whole life in fear and trembling? Let your heart bleed at last, and speak! How stupid a head was as a mere head, no matter how big—the bigger, the worse. Son of a king mustn't ride alone. The lady sat two lance-lengths away. Woman without a name can't be married. And no door was locked anywhere in the town during her nuptials. But no one knew that he still had much farther to ride. The unmatched loneliness of a proud woman! And soon both felt at home in their exhaustion. No tears, hero of our time: when you weep, you're done for. A love without fear and trembling is a fire without warmth. May your heart burst in your belly, knight. And may Aaron strike it with his rod, and may it become a cliff— may Moses break his commandment anew from this cliff. You must travel all roads, or the adventure will never be brought to an end. And at the king's court you must wait. But the most beautiful thing that happened to them in the end was a beautiful reception. — My place: with my face pointing down. There will be a wind, and I shall be no more. At bottom every day of my life was a shame and a disgrace—the only thing I'm proud of is the nights when I stayed up. The inky cap lies in its ink, the bleeder in his blood. You didn't realize how tall the tree was until a person perched in its crown." — And at that he had his hand shaken by the long-time poet as well.

He then gave both of them money and watched as they drove off in his car, the poet at the wheel, starting up with a jerk, then another. And that same afternoon he set out himself across the steppe that began at the end of the street. He'd already ventured onto it by day, in wide arcs, returning to town each time toward evening. Now the tie that had always pulled him back to Santa Fe was broken, and his destination lay somewhere else entirely. And for the first time in his story the direction was also clear: to the northwest.

According to the calendar at the inn, it was supposed to be a new moon. But in broad daylight there appeared in the firmament a sickle; the calendar was one from the year before.

My storyteller struck out energetically, away from civilization for the time being. He strode energetically out onto the steppe. A thousand roads you must travel, or your adventure will never be brought to an end!

As on his exploratory excursions, he took off his sunglasses as soon as he got past the houses and out into the grassland, not only because the light was less harsh here than among the houses, most of which had white stucco, but also because the details out here had a different effect on him without them. Not for a moment did he use his dark glasses in the period that followed, even during the most glaring midday. Besides, hadn't he already taken every step once before, in just this way? Or had that been his ancestors? Which one of them? King Gilgamesh, the steppe-runner? And simultaneously, just as every time in the past when he felt he'd already experienced something or other, it seemed to mean a great danger was looming over him.

The town at his back was still very much with him—cranes, power saws, jackhammers. Yet with the first step from the end of the paved road onto the savanna, he entered a different sound-realm. His actual footsteps suddenly became almost inaudible—as if he'd passed a tipping point or a sort of sound-divide—or at least they were no more pronounced than the thousands of other sounds in the grass—like taking off your shoes while walking.

Yet "grass" and "grassland" weren't really accurate. This particular highland steppe—but wasn't every steppe unique—consisted not so much of grasses as of late-summer-dry herbs and thistles, and, in between, patches of fairly friable soil, like deposits of rubble or ash; or each spot on the steppe was reminiscent of a buried road. And indeed, far into the area, glass shards, pieces of porcelain, bottle stoppers, and the like were sticking out of the ground. A single nut tree was growing there, with already cracked shells, into which he dug for a first bit of nourishment. The steppe's predominant color was gray, silver-veil-gray. And there were no smells until he plunged both hands into the gray-faded chamomile, the anise stalks, the likewise gray-faded tufts of lavender. But the aftersmell was still there when he told me his story the following winter.

· · ·

For quite a while he walked backward through the steppe, casting a few farewell glances at the town of the nocturnal wind. Not so much the houses there contrasted with the surroundings here as the suddenly vibrant green strips along the rivers that merged down below, with their vegetable gardens and stands of poplars. Without the rays of sun striking the very tips of the poplars—the only parts of the lower town still reached by the sun—the region would have appeared to him shrouded in a uniform gloom. A distant hammering was multiplied by the echo-cliffs, and the sound bounced off them as if very close by, while all of it sounded like muezzins' calls from the town's minarets—many, very many. At the same time, beneath his backward footsteps, the scattering in all directions of myriads of gray grasshoppers, a flicking-away-sound like that of fingernail-clipping.

All right! Onward! He made a 180-degree turn. After all, he was out on the steppe in order to bring something back from there. To whom? To whomever. Simply to bring something back. He was still wearing his work clothes, by now faded to a pale blue, a roomy smock and wide trousers. Now he also tied a cloth around his forehead as protection against the sun. As he pulled it tight, his eyebrows were caught as well, and it felt as though his eyes were being tightened. And in fact he was seeing more distinctly. Although the ocean was almost a thousand steppe miles away, ocean blue rose above the nearest horizon.

· · ·

He walked until evening without coming upon any adventure, not even a larger animal. The largest he saw was an eagle, spiraling toward the savanna, its wings two almost-open knife blades, and in its wake for a while a squadron of deep-black sparkling town-cliff jackdaws, which, while the eagle uttered at most a monosyllabic croak now and then, emitted salvos of cries that resounded rhythmically through the air, a chorus of cracking whips overhead.

He, however, kept his eyes fixed in front of him, mostly on the ground, in search of special steppe mushrooms, preferably bitter ones—if he was an expert on anything, then on bitter mushrooms—for his mushroom book, which he wanted to finish at last when he got home, but also because that felt better for the time being. Almost the only time he looked up or turned his head was when he heard the sound of a car on that vast prairie, far from any roads (only a very finicky car would have needed a real road there). During his first hours out walking, a couple of cars did pass him, at more or less great distances, and each time it was another of those Santana all-terrain vehicles, of which there was apparently an inexhaustible variety of sizes and shapes. Later he noticed that this kind of carefree rolling across the steppe merely appeared to be that; in actuality, the drivers had to be on the lookout for the crevasses created by the occasional brooks, some of them as deep as gorges, and drive around them, just as he circumvented them on foot.

On the other hand, he didn't turn to look when, as still happened during the first hour, runners came panting up behind him; initially tempted while still ahead of them to speed up, as they did, he then slowed down instead. Nor did he look up for the cross-steppe-bicyclists, who usually stormed by in herds on their bazooka-width tires, preceded from afar on the meanwhile treeless grasslands by a shouting and crashing; they remained his most persistent companions, all the way into the areas with nothing but crickets chirping on all sides: He didn't need to look at these helmeted, swaddled faces and streamlined figures shooting back to nature, under whose tires anything living was splintered, uprooted, squashed, or lost its just-established foothold in the soil. And each of these riders evidently considered himself the very embodiment of adventure. But this wasn't the adventure he was seeking.

Before sunset, alone with the steppe at last. A "larger animal" meanwhile turned up after all: an ownerless dog who lived in a hole in the ground and accompanied him for a long while, at first baring its teeth, later licking his fingers. Now it grew so quiet that he involuntarily cupped his hand to his ear to catch the few almost imperceptible sounds, mostly from inside the earth. When a breath of wind passed through the dry vegetation, it produced a slight ringing, like the sound of onionskin pages being turned.

Yes, he'd been in this area once before, a very long time ago, and, as he now felt in every fiber of his being, not alone. And soon he would be needing a place to spend the night, but as he shaded his eyes against the last sun, as far as the most distant cloud-shadow over the landscape, as it were, that shadow there as motionless as the few others, he saw not a sign of human habitation. And at the same time, at his feet, in the pathless waste, under a tangle of blackberries, there appeared an almost vanished steppe-milestone or signpost, according to which he was not all that far from "Los Jerónimos." On the other hand, hadn't he already passed a sign announcing the village of "Los Lobos" (the wolves)—but the village itself was missing, and likewise a "Weymar"—and after that nothing, nothing at all.

Here, however, the crowing of roosters could be heard, and even something that sounded like turkeys gobbling. He headed toward it, and found himself entering a previously hidden valley, nothing there but a chapel in ruins and a garden with a shed next to it. He hadn't been out on the savanna all that long, and already he'd acquired a different gait, a broad stride, slightly pigeon-toed, snow-plow-like. At the garden entrance a hedgehog hobbled by, something he hadn't seen in a long while, but now, with the sun setting, in the moment before its disappearance, suddenly appearing huge and primeval, "the biggest animal on my entire trip."

At the time when this story takes place, Europe had more and more hermits again. One was also living in the steppe valley, and he gave the storyteller a place to spend the night. He was offered something to eat and a bed in the ancient caravan behind the ruined chapel.

Neither of the two had opened his mouth, and not until the next morning, with the whistling of the coffee water, did it become clear that the hermit was deaf. Now my storyteller noticed the resemblance between this man and someone who had once been a good friend of his and mine, the vanished classics teacher from Salzburg, Andreas Loser. Yes, it was him. But they both acted as though they didn't know each other—

except that the hermit fetched out that "Blue Mountain" coffee from Jamaica. So of the three of us, the one who had depended primarily on listening and hearing had become deaf, perhaps precisely from the eternal silence of the steppe?! And in a part of the country that was called, of all things, the "Sabana de la Sonora"? "Even from that one night there," my storyteller said, "my ears were overwhelmed; it passed so soundlessly, with even the rooster and the turkey silent, and upon awakening I wanted to rub a file over the hermitage bell, so as to have something to hear—anything."

"Did that Loser at least do what a hermit's supposed to—cut some grass for your horse?"

"Yes. And by the way, during my entire time on the steppe it felt as if I, though actually on foot, were galloping along on horseback."

As he continued onward, what disturbed him at first was constantly seeing his shadow in front of him, for the eastern sun was at his back. For that reason, too, he walked backward again for a while. But later he observed the individual details on the ground, which appeared more distinctly in his shadow. And toward noon the shadow was almost out of sight in any case; he now welcomed having it in the corners of his eyes, for in the relative sameness of the steppe, from horizon to horizon, it provided a sense of forward motion and of being unobtrusively accompanied.

And so he went on for days. He never came upon a village. But there wasn't a day when he remained constantly

PETER HANDKE

alone. One time he saw, far off, as if on another path through
the steppe, a figure pulling a cart. The figure turned in his
direction, and then he heard a few measures of music, as if
from a flute, but more shrill, also carrying farther, piercing, the
melody repeated ceaselessly. The wanderer was a peddler, who,
on a metal rod with holes punched in it, announced his presence, welcome to the storyteller, for in the meantime his
shoelaces, both of them, had broken. On the peddler's cart, the
word ULTRAMARINOS was written in large letters, which was
actually supposed to mean "overseas wares." — Or the peddler
turned up merely to shine his shoes—but how!

One afternoon he lay down for a nap on a stretch of prairie
with the tall grass providing shadow, and when he then
scrambled to his feet, next to him something heavy suddenly
leaped into the air, with a howl—again a stray dog that
had probably wandered onto the steppe as a puppy and had
been lying there asleep, with each of them oblivious of the
other, just inches away in the waist-high grass, but the dog
now fleeing, frightened, from what seemed to be its established hollow. And on the houseless steppe gray chicks likewise fled from him, first at a deliberate pace, then suddenly
speeding up and arrowing crookedly into the air, a whole
colony of quail, at which a couple of hunters promptly
fired, seemingly springing up out of the ground over here and
over there.

And one morning a runner came toward him—from
where?—the fabric over his chest one big patch of sweat, and
moving even faster than a runner anywhere else; then, once
past him, turned, blocking his path, and had a gun in his hand,

yet was no hunter: Aiming at him and releasing the safety catch, he accused him of raping his wife and ordered him to come along for a lineup, but then a glance at the few mushrooms on the other's palm, and he was off, running without a word, in an entirely different direction this time.

And once, toward evening, he came upon a small group, a young woman on horseback and on one side of her an almost childlike soldier with a fairly tattered uniform and on the other a medieval man in a long, open dustcoat, on one shoulder a small, tiger-striped, yellow-eyed peregrine falcon, on the other, squeezed under the coat's clasp, a deck of playing cards, and he was asked whether he'd perhaps seen an old man, lost and probably mentally confused, one who wrote in the air as he walked and now and then took a little hop, grotesque for a man of his age; they had been out searching for him for weeks but didn't want to come home without him, alive or dead. Afterward, although he'd merely shaken his head curtly in reply to their question and continued on his way, it seemed to him that the man they were seeking had crossed his path after all, and just recently, and he subsequently brooded all night as to where and in what manner that had happened: No, he hadn't seen him, also hadn't heard or smelled him—he would have been sure of the latter—but? Perhaps, simply from the urgency the little rescue party projected, he'd formed a sort of phantom image of the man they were looking for.

And not just once, but now a thousand-times-a-thousand steppe paces farther west, did he hear again a few piercing, far-carrying steel-rod measures, and again the Ultramarinos cart with the steppe peddler turned off course to meet him and offered him exactly what he most needed or wished for, even if that was now an apple, now a bandage.

He walked as straight ahead as possible. If he got off track, it was out of the question to turn around, to make his way back to the point where he'd gone wrong. What mattered was pressing steadily onward and forward, even if this resulted in having insurmountable obstacles stand in the way of resuming his direction. A detour—perhaps (if it was a small one). But not one step back—with the exception of going forward by walking backward!

And sometimes he cut off even the most natural detours as if instinctively. Thus he slithered down the banks of gorges, fell, and tumbled head-over-heels, and not just once. He became almost addicted to such moments of sliding faster and faster, in the midst of which he now and then sniffed a tuft of thyme as it zoomed by, picked a few blackberries and popped them in his mouth, committed to memory the pattern of wood-worm tunnels in a barkless branch.

Probably not remarkable that his senses were sharpened by such exposures to danger. Except that the impressions lingered for a long time, and for that reason, too, he didn't try to avoid them even once. Precisely the fear that didn't spare him during the stumbling and falling opened the eyes of this man who'd wearied of the journey at least once a day, opened them in such a way that afterward, as he continued on firm ground, he took in the steppe in more than panoramic format.

"And there was nothing missing," my storyteller said. "But just when I thought nothing was missing, sometimes everything was missing. For that reason, after a while I came to prefer that refreshing of the present moment and the day by means of frightening experiences to everything else. I realized, you see, that now and then, when I was particularly full of what I was encountering on my journey, I'd begun to narrate the story, in secret, not purposefully. Perhaps to no one in particular—or maybe that wasn't true, after all?—but certainly not to myself. This storytelling extended as far as the steppe all around me. And precisely the contrast between such moments and those when my thoughts were somewhere else entirely, when I was worrying, wrangling with myself or the world, or, worst of all, was also inwardly mute—this contrast revealed to me what was most significant: When I inadvertently fell into such storytelling my thoughts weren't actually elsewhere, even when the storytelling dealt with something absent and removed; I was actually taking in my surroundings more acutely than in and after a situation of danger. And if not more acutely, then more colorfully and richly. The things inside me and outside of me interpenetrated each other, became whole from one another. Storytelling and the steppe became one. So this was the right place. This type of storytelling produced a sense of discovery, created transitions, made one look up, also in the sense of looking up to something, a bird's-eye view, an eagle's-eye view!"

One time he spent the night in a steppe garage, next to one of the fragmentary landing strips. In addition to a bar, it also had a sleeping nook. Another time he slept in a garrison surrounded by watchtowers and barbed wire, another time in a long abandoned little steppe railway building, amidst the piled-up junk there (which recovered during the night, however, and went back where it belonged).

He slept soundly and dreamlessly every time, if not for long. A previously unknown impatience roused him from his sleep—impatience to get going again across the steppe. He lay there in the new-moon darkness and couldn't see why it took so long in this region for a first sign of day to appear. He cursed the darkness, unchanging for hours, yet so palpably spacious and promising. Where were they, the first light and the first birds of day? Enough of the owls' hooting.

In that garage berth he'd eventually turned on the light, switched on a television set, tried to read a grease-smeared newspaper: But the newspaper called *The Santa Fe Day*—so he was still in the large province of the nocturnal-wind town— bore a date from the previous spring, and the television news was from the day before yesterday and the day after tomorrow. And this one time when he couldn't wait to continue across the savanna but set out while it was still dark, groping his way in the pitch black, had exhausted him so much that for the rest of the day he couldn't get his eyes open properly.

As time went on, instead of the signs for towns, crooked, half buried in the scree (the towns themselves completely buried), like "Santa Ana," "San Juan," or "San Francisco," he found himself wishing for a sign that would read "Santa Paciencia." He would never have thought he could tire of gazing at the con- stellations, for instance the sparkling image of the huntsman Orion, spangled across the sky, and meanwhile, with fall approaching, visible every night; yet now he looked up at it only in order to see all those stars fade with the dawn, including those representing the huntsman's knees, belt, and quiver— first the quiver disappeared, then—it was time—the first of the three belt stars, and the most stubbornly persistent were one of the two shoulder stars, and even more so, the last to disappear from the day, the glittering knee-star Aldebaran. "Ah, finally gone, the sky empty—a sign for being able to get under way!"

But a closer look detected another flash emanating from the huntsman Orion, with daylight almost there; even the belt and quiver leaped forth from the sky's brightness, or weren't those black residual images? Santa Paciencia!

"The first step onto the soil of the steppe always brought a fresh sense of excitement," he said, "the transition from the concrete, asphalt, paved, hardened surfaces in front of the garage, the barracks, the railroad station, the abandoned cattle shed, and into and down to and up to this ground under your feet, where the springy effect immediately set in, relieving the body of so much that weighed it down. How lightly you floated along, almost too lightly. For that reason, too, I put stones in my pockets, and now understood better the poet who once said that he ate so much, or in general took in so much, because he hoped in that way not to get rid of his state of constant agitation but to load it down with gravity."

Could it be that such a condition was even intensified by the smells that wafted up at him from the ground, which was that of a particular aromatic herb-steppe? — "Yes, but these aromas were by no means the main intensifiers. Toward the end of the day they even gave me headaches every time, close to nausea. There was such a wealth of them, and from plant to plant such gradations, distinctions, refinements, and refinements of refinements, that I imagined all of them together should yield a tincture or essence such as had never been smelled or tasted before, and that I absolutely had to bring home with me—with healing powers simply because, without instructions or urging, it made you breathe deeply. An essence in another sense, in time I absorbed something else entirely from the world of steppe plants: Nowhere could you find, in bloom or bearing fruit, those things, which, probably lasting far into summer, would have made for an utterly different steppe, at least to judge by the infinite range of dull yellow to dull gray dried puffs, balls, tufts, and strands atop all the tall stalks, stems, and shafts. Even the fruits and the withered remains of flowers had burst for the most part, fallen off, and blown away. Of the transhorizontal sea of blossoms and small fruits, almost all that remained were the things that provided stability and protection to the petals, anthers, pistils, and the like: the stems, of course, and additionally and in particular the sepals, the blossoms' empty bottoms and supports, the empty fruit capsules and husks. Myriads of flower and fruit skeletons, from small to minuscule, often also dull brown and chalky white, poked up all across the steppe from their likewise bleached, gangly stalks, with an incredible wealth of forms—cylinders, spirals, gears, combs, also threes, eights, and nines on these miniature skeletons! It was these infinitely many and extraordinarily varied little steppe-plant skeletons that leaped out at me as an essence such as you seldom find. I felt as though tiny vegetative skeletons like these revealed an entire vanished and swallowed-up world that you could study anew. For here it wasn't the case that 'vanished' also meant 'evaporated.' The empty lavender skeletons smelled of lavender—and how. The empty poppy capsules were redolent of poppy seeds—and how. The bare caraway stalks smelled more powerfully of caraway than ever. And added to this was another smell, which simply came from the hundreds of empty shapes, the essence, to be precise. In observing and inhaling the dear little skeletons—yes, I felt a sort of tenderness for them—and also in listening (for instance to the rattling of the capsules), I became conscious of my own bone structure, and I can't say it horrified me. Bending over the plant remains, I experienced for moments at a time an epiphany, and where did I feel it? — In my bones. And must I add that after a day like this, at night in my sleeping place, I was amazed to have gotten out alive from such a deadly sinister steppe?

"And since I'm speaking so boldly now," said the pharmacist of Taxham, "I'm going to tell you briefly about myself and the steppe mushrooms. Only briefly: because my passion for mushrooms estranged my wife from me, and I don't want to lose my scribe as well! Let's get it over with, so we can move on with my story. On the other hand, I also want to mention quickly that I'm convinced the last conversational topic human beings will have in common, aside from current events in the newspaper and on television, will be the various types of mushrooms—the last subject on which everyone will agree, even total strangers, pricking up their ears, amicably. Perhaps the last shared adventure available to all of us nowadays, also because it's so hard to describe. Yet inexhaustible. Like the steppe, also hard to describe because resistant to images. And my mushroom book will be one that will make people exclaim: Yes, that's just how it is, that's what I've always said, too!—even if they've never said it.

"And the fact was that with all the rich discoveries of plants and rocks on the steppe, I had the sense of making a real discovery only with the mushrooms. Along the way I even bit off, or at least stuck under my tongue, pieces of even the inedible or poisonous ones—yes, that's how stale I often felt from being alone and mute: I wanted acidity for my mouth, and especially bitterness for my tongue, and the bitterest mushrooms were exactly what I needed. Some were so bitter that the bitterness hit me again, from inside. In my mushroom book I'm going to make a point of recommending a couple of bitter mushrooms like that, for eating raw. But the good steppe mushrooms, the sweet ones: how they opened my eyes!"

"And?" I asked.

The pharmacist: "Yes, isn't that enough for a start? The mere sight of them woke me up."

"The way his prey wakes up the hunter?"

"Yes, maybe. Except that the mushrooms didn't run away from me, but on the contrary seemed to be waiting for me: At last you've found me! To be sure, it wasn't good if there were too many; too much splendor overstimulated and dulled me. — And another thing, but then that'll be all I say about mushrooms for now and in this context: In them I smelled all my kin again—my father, my mother, my grandparents; above all, my children, when they were still children."

Later came days when my storyteller was no longer looking for anything at all as he made his way across the steppe. And it felt to him like a kind of freedom—"which I wouldn't have found without the searching that preceded it."

On the top of a hill someone was sitting, fishing in the air. Thistle flowers far below on the ground were black sea urchins at the same time. For one whole windless day, clouds of pollen billowed from the male elderberry bushes to the female elderberry bushes—so there were still blossoms after all on the autumnal steppe? — Yes. In a pine forest—so there were forests, too, on the steppe?—there was a particular cone-eating-tree for the squirrels (just as in cities there are sleeping-trees for birds); the needle-covered ground blanketed as if with the remains of apples. And the high grasses there—one place on the steppe with only grasses—nodded and shook their heads at the same time. A cloud field, white, rippled, foamy, forming dunes. Flat oval stones here and there on top of the highland scree, with a black circle in the middle: pebbles polished by the Ice Age, which had sunk into the ocean here as the snows melted, called "eye stones."

Even when he blew with all his might on the small and smallest steppe animals that lighted on him, they stayed put. One night, in the coolness, he stuck both hands into a bovist he had picked during the day, the size of a bull's skull and deep reddish black—what a mushroom!—and let the sun's warmth inside flow into him: It worked. A single butterfly wing was moving along the ground, upright, wobbling slightly and in a zigzag, multicolored, like a military standard: carried by a cave-black ant. And the ants here didn't seem to form a state anywhere—at most three or four would come out of a hole at a time; so only little ant villages and hamlets, which were located far apart and had nothing to do with each other.

Wasps zoomed around like everywhere else, only close to the ground here. And one time a large grasshopper ("hay-horse" was the Austrian word) was carrying a smaller grasshopper on its back, whereupon the latter fell off and hopped around looking for its carrier. And then the two of them, one atop the other again, displayed profiles that actually resembled horses, while the steppe moths had the profiles of sheep. One of the moths, stone-gray, was fluttering next to a cliff, also gray, and was visible only because at the same time its shadow was moving over the cliff.

From time to time he saw beehives lined up on the steppe—mostly next to another such cliff—which produced a constant hum, and upon the bees' returning and slipping into the dark holes, their little pollen-dusted legs glowed—"So there was still something in bloom after all?"—and whenever he passed a little colony like that he was immediately attacked by an animal that came shooting out at him, the watchman or people's policeman on duty, and was usually also stung, regularly on his cheekbone.

Little patches of green, surrounded by the tall, sparse steppe vegetation, not visible until you were standing directly in front of them, were wild vegetable gardens, with sorrel and something reminiscent of dandelion greens, only fatter, softer, and more juicy, but, like dandelion greens, slightly bitter. "I've hardly ever eaten such delicacies as I did there," he told me, "of course just small things, but all the more delicate. And for a change, I didn't read at all, or only this way: The steppe, the villages were my library."

Then fewer and fewer beehives, and the bees creeping into them also had less and less yellow on their feet. And finally their back legs were completely free of pollen. And likewise, the blackberries he still managed to find were all only half ripe; the other half was green and wouldn't ripen any more. But at the same time a magnolia was in bloom next to the ruins of a steppe house—a spring tree, as if blossoming for the first time that year.

The prevailing impression, however, especially in the island-like pine groves, where a ceaseless swishing of needles could be heard, was that of the days just before spring. And on a sunny, rather cool day like that, he was resting in late afternoon in a spot by a clay-yellow, almost vegetationless little slope, sheltered from the wind, a bank, of which there was a duplicate behind him: He was stretched out there between the two banks as if on the bed of a sunken road. He was lying on his side, the needle-strewn ground beneath him, from which here and there a plant poked, always consisting of only one leaf, thin as sheet metal, atop a naked stalk, and the leaves gave off a metallic clanging.

He had an unobstructed view of the clay wall, close enough to touch. The wall was hollowed out lengthwise, forming a kind of niche, and he thought this niche, with the soft clay dust and a bed of pine needles, would have made a good place for spending the night. He had nothing before his eyes but the red-gray-yellow fissured surface of the earth, illuminated by the last sun, now low in the sky.

He'd always been drawn most powerfully to observation when he witnessed the simplest, most undramatic occurrences and processes, for instance rain coming down heavier or tapering off, or simply continuing; snow melting; a puddle slowly drying up. And thus he also observed the shallow clay semi-grotto lit by the last rays of the sun.

It was in fact a form of lighting, seeming almost artificial, like that of a spotlight or film projector: Every detail of the earthen wall emerged clearly—grainy, furrowed, like a relief. From the hair roots of trees sticking out here and there hung clumps of clay and also a few shreds of moss, from which only now, as the sunlight reached them, for the only time that day, the morning dew was vanishing. (There was a lot of dew on the steppe, though clinging almost exclusively to birds' feathers and the few mossy spots, but all the more concentrated there, making the moss cushions serviceable as sponges.)

The only thing that diverted his attention at first was the lone shell casing from a hunter's gun, covered entirely by spiderwebs, including the interior—that was how long it had been lodged in the sand. And he left it there, as if it belonged. And then he also left himself. He left himself behind. And at first he lay there without breathing; didn't need to for a while.

The earthen niche, its smooth portions more and more lamplight-yellow, its fissured and raised surfaces more and more shadow-black, did his tired eyes good, more than anything green would have. It could also have been the side of a mountain, in some primeval time, beyond or at least outside of any recorded history, and there was the sense of lying stretched out by this prehistoric mountain range, extending almost as far as it did. The current wars were taking place far off on the other side. Sand seeped out of the clay, sand avalanches hurtled toward the valley. How old this world was. Or how young? Just at its beginning, or even before that? The concave vein of clay seemed not to be lit up by the sunset but rather lit from within; it radiated light, was its source. And the clay, displaying every shade of yellow, was the embodiment of light. Dear ancestors. Dear Father. Dear Mother.

From a hole in the clay poked a dragon's head, a cricket, with an abrupt sustained chirping, while on top of the bank a steppe hunter appeared with his gun, and took aim at him as he lay there, whereupon down on the sunken road my story-teller's double appeared, promptly shot dead by the hunter. And a grasshopper then took a leap in the air and went from hopping to flying, as he, too, sometimes managed to do, though only in dreams. As it took off, the insect had extended blue wings from under its gray shell, and during its flight had appeared blue all over, but once it landed it promptly became stone-gray again.

From the other side of the sunken road an all-terrain vehicle appeared, another Santana, decorated with streamers for a wedding, which stopped right by him, the driver the storyteller's son, with his bride, the young festival queen. And his son bent down to him and said, "You didn't throw me out, Father. I'm the one who went away, of my own accord. I left you, for good. And that's what you wanted." And he felt he had to reply to his son: "I've incurred great guilt, irreparable guilt!" but he couldn't get out a single word, whereupon the newlyweds slowly drove on, waving to him. And now a cascade of chestnuts, hard as rocks and just as heavy, rattled down onto the road, striking everywhere but on his head, just where he needed them—and then his child was gone, vanished, and they would never see each other again.

He lay there, weary unto death, facing the groove where he had just had a glimpse of the Creation. His time was up. There was no escaping from this wall now. A snail's shell jerked oddly along at the foot of the clay wall, as if empty, stood still, rolled on, and continued this way until he saw that periodically a wasp, its yellow hardly visible against the yellow of the clay, would dart down and give it a push, moving the shell forward in its efforts to pull out the snail cadaver. And another wasp had just seized a bee and was rolling around with it in the dust. And as he lay there, he dug out a mushroom that had just emerged from the clay of the ground; when he wanted to break it loose, it proved too heavy for him, indeed became heavier and heavier, and pulled the man who was trying to lift it down into the earth instead, which under the mushroom was hollow—increasing blackness and finally bottomlessness.

And now he broke out in a cold sweat of death. Was there really such a thing? Yes. This cold sweat was more viscous than normal sweat, and came out of all his pores, a sort of water that cut a person off from the external world and prevented the skin from breathing.

And now a shadow appeared on the clay wall lit by the late afternoon sun, not a hard shadow but the shadow of someone who unhurriedly, cautiously, came up behind him and squatted at his back, the shadow of a woman, the most beautiful shadow he'd ever encountered—never had he seen such a kind, warm-hearted shadow!

And this woman's shadow now said the following to him: "Stop seeking the living here among the dead! You will shake off your speechlessness. Otherwise your not speaking will do you in this very day. Your silence is no mere taciturnity. It's true that at first, and then for a while afterward, it enlarged the world for you. But the longer you remained alone this way, the more your muteness became a threat to you, and finally life-threatening. Your continued muteness not only makes the present unreal to you, no matter how significant it may appear to you in a given moment, but is also retroactively destroying everything you experienced in the past, even the most significant things—all the way back to childhood. It devalues and destroys your memory, without which you have no business being in the world, and makes you in-significant. You have reached the outer limits of the world, my friend. And you are in danger of ending up beyond the confines of the world. Therefore you will have to make an effort at regaining speech, at recovering words, at recreating sentences, out loud, at least audibly. And even if your speaking is dead wrong and ridiculous: the main thing is to open your mouth. And this very evening, down there in Saragossa. I need your help. Yes, you heard me right: I need your help. But to be able to help me you must open your mouth again!"

A blow on the back of his head, this time positively tender. And the woman's shadow disappeared. And when he turned around, there was no one there. And now he had to get away from the steppe.

Now he was in a hurry. He, of all people? Yes. Something he had hardly ever done: He broke into a run.

And now it was downhill all the way. Occasionally he would also leap, without hesitating. Even when something he'd lost long ago flashed up at him, he snatched it from beneath his feet and ran on at once (yet he'd lost this thing—he didn't say what it was—somewhere else entirely—had a raven served as the transporter again?).

At this speed, his perceptions were even sharper. The steppe lizards, no bigger than a person's little finger, tailless, scurried away, into the fissures of the rock. The only snake he came upon during that entire time, as thick as an arm and grayish-black, shot with a rattle up a pine trunk that was also grayish-black, and remained there in the exact position of the pharmacy emblem, and both of them, the man here and the snake dangling in the tree there, had the same gaze: out of the corners of their eyes, fixed.

Moths then flew up like dust from the gray of the steppe, the moth the same gray as the steppe, but when one of these late butterflies spread its wings, they were translucent, incised on the inner surface with a moon, stars, planetary orbits, and somewhat resembling stained-glass windows, not medieval but modern ones. Meanwhile the air was abuzz with universal signals, coming from small cracks and holes in the earth: toad calls and cricket chirps. A few bats zigzagged by, and he became aware of how much he'd missed them. He wouldn't turn back again. "Better to die than to turn back!"

One of the first signs of the city was a couple of cross-steppe bicyclists, shooting downhill with brakes screeching from horizon to horizon. "With the stick I had with me, I killed them as I ran past," my storyteller said, "and since then the steppe's been more or less free of this plague." Another sign of the city's proximity: the found objects, smaller and larger, scooped up from the ground, which he tossed as far ahead of him as he could in his unceasing forward motion, to give himself boost after boost—at first mostly rocks or sticks, these more and more replaced by empty bottles, tin cans, batteries, and chunks of brick.

Before a final ridge, with the city beyond it, and probably way below it, still not visible at all, he heard from the distance a thousand-voiced singing, a chorale, which seemed to come from a monumental cloister: It turned out to be the cars, zooming by on the highway one right behind the other, the evening rush hour.

The first glimpse he got of the city was the airport down below, at his feet, with the landing lights on the runways pointing like fingers into the distance, and in the sky above it a traffic helicopter, seemingly hovering in one place, its lights flashing, while he stood there, directly across from the bulky machine, at the same altitude, in the high steppe grass, holding a steppe potato he'd snatched up somewhere, and at his back, above the deserted expanse, the waxing, almost lightless moon, while before him, to the left and right, lay the highway and, crossing it, the railroad tracks: back to the spandrel world.

At least he hadn't been going in a circle the whole time. For this city was situated completely differently from his point of departure, Santa Fe: It was still on the steppe characteristic of all of Spain, but in the lowlands, where the herb steppe gave way to a gone-to-seed savanna; and that was fine: no more headache. And upon arriving, he'd blown out the blockage in his ears. Although this city was just a provincial capital, you could have fit ten Santa Fes or nocturnal-wind towns into it, and was it simply another coincidence that it was called Saragossa? No, this was the real Saragossa, with the Ebro River far off there in the lowland background.

Now it was a matter of getting across this large city of Saragossa, all the way to the road leading out of the city in the north. And he'd been walking so long already that he wanted to keep going this way to the end, and straight ahead.

What turned out to be a problem were not the distances but the obstacles in all directions. Thus he had another adventure: To get from the country-wide steppe into the spandrel world of the present, on foot, could be quite adventurous, even more adventurous than finding your way out of it on foot.

And besides, he'd made a bet with himself: that he'd see if he could stay as much as possible on the steppe, even on his way through the city, until he reached his destination; here in Spain that wasn't inconceivable, in his experience. But the steppe was preserved primarily in the in-between patches created by the various transportation lines. And so he scrambled over highway barriers, waited for that one moment in a hundred when you could reach the other shore, running and jumping; in the same fashion he crossed the railway embankment, then had the next loop of the highway to get over, then the airport, then the second rail line, the local one, always by way of crabgrass spandrels, almost bare, getting narrower and narrower, more pointed, smaller, and so on, deep into the city and then almost all the way out again.

"I won't add any more details here," my storyteller said, "but if some day you want to write a very modern adventure book, it should be about a journey on foot from out in the open country—where that still exists—into the cities."

As far as his own adventure was concerned, he mentioned only the many animals he came upon while crossing the spandrels, all the more as the space grew narrower, more hemmed in by the transportation lines, and also more species, more varied. The very ones he'd been missing on the steppe, the larger breeds, he encountered here on these tiny islands of savanna, shrinking more and more toward the center of the city, and finally enclosed like cages, which as a rule had the shape of triangles, with increasingly acute angles, in the end reduced to no more than a line: There, and nowhere out on the steppe, crouched the hares, massive, and next to them, fearless, stood the occasional fox by its burrow, likewise a white weasel—as if they all knew that in their grassy enclosures, railed and embanked in, they were sheltered from any eyes, except perhaps from above, from airplanes.

Although he merely brushed the center of Saragossa, he realized that there, as when he'd arrived in the nocturnal-wind town, a festival was in progress. The doors of the many churches were opened wide, the interiors brightly lit, in contrast to the shops, which were all closed (among them most conspicuously the pharmacies—his eye sought them out—for here in the city, unlike in Santa Fe earlier, all of them had their iron shutters rolled down).

Yes, it was the annual festival of the patron saint of Saragossa, Nuestra Señora del Pilar, Our Lady of the Pillar. That meant it must be almost mid-October by now? So he'd already been away from home so long?

He ran faster, as if he could make up for lost time that way. He had no eyes for this festival. And from another side street he suddenly heard the sound of the steel-rod flute, even shriller here among the city buildings than out on the steppe, frenetic, rising above the rooftops, the unvarying sequence of notes repeated at intervals determined by a few steps and pushes of the peddler's cart, also wilder, unfettered, bold, and at the same time expressing an obsequious politeness and distance-preserving formality, for after all, the peddler wanted to do business, holiday or no. What mattered to the itinerant sales-man was not music but crying and offering his wares. The sound penetrated all the commotion of the festival.

So the peddler had made the same journey as he had, straight across one province and then into the other, and then another, and now, after all those weeks, with each moving along in his own way, they'd reached the metropolis at the same moment.

The piercing sound continued, in a distant parallel alley, and always level with him, heading toward the Río Ebro. And for the first time in his story, for the first time altogether—in how long?—tears came to his eyes. And at that moment he wanted to go straight to the peddler and buy something from him.

But then they ran into each other anyway on the Puente Piedra, and he had the peddler sharpen his knife for him.

Meanwhile night had fallen, and Saragossa revealed itself as a nocturnal-wind town like the other one. He went to his pre-arranged rendezvous: instead of to some palace of the kings of Navarra, to a bus station on the outskirts of town, beyond and to the north of the Ebro.

Although he didn't feel tired, now and then his knees gave way under him. The bus station was a sprawling structure without walls at the end of a road leading out of the city, lined with apartment houses on one side, holding back the beginning of a new expanse of empty steppe on the other. The station roof was supported by a large number of thick, round concrete columns, each of which marked the departure gate for the various destinations: Huesca, Lérida, Tudela, and even more distant ones, beyond the Pyrenees. At their base, the columns were surrounded by pedestals. Although there was a glassed-in, well-lit waiting area, the pedestals were occupied by passengers, on each of the more than two dozen pedestals usually just one passenger—a different sort of pillar event from the festival in town. Quite a few passengers were also standing, leaning their backs against the columns.

He sat down on his pedestal, the one closest to the road, where the breeze from the passing trucks buffeted him. The buses pulling into the station shrank by contrast with the rows of columns to the size of small vehicles, and emerged from there as giants again. The apartment houses along the road seemed almost depopulated. Apparently this festival was one of those that focus more on particular parts of town, so the others seemed all the more deserted. Shreds of plastic fluttered toward the outskirts. Balls of thistle spores, silvery, floated toward town, together with the tangles of briars familiar from the steppe, which rolled along the ground, occasionally skipping. Was time no longer passing?

And now he felt a hand on his shoulder, warm and gentle as almost never before. And likewise another hand was placed on his brow, and another hand. Many hands placed themselves on him, and then also draped a coat over his shoulders—he was freezing. And now the woman, his pursuer, said, "So, you're asleep."

The vehicle that had come to a halt in front of him, its folding doors open, inviting him to enter, was not a Santana all-terrain vehicle, also not the almost bus-length Santana he had seen before, but a real bus, in no way different from the others in the station, except that no one rode off in it but the two of them, she at the wheel, and he next to her, on that isolated seat seemingly meant for a tour guide, which swiveled and was considerably lower than hers.

Here he now sat, facing backward, for the entire time they were on the road together; at night he fixed his gaze on the empty rows of seats, by day also on the areas receding from view and even more on those that from this perspective came into view, not to be seen ahead of time but only when the bus was level with them: their individual features easier to grasp in their context, appearing first large, then growing smaller as they receded. Or was such a position—facing backward—a matter of growing older? "At any rate," my storyteller said, "I resolved that if I should ever again in my life set out across the continents, I would sit facing away from the direction in which I was traveling, if possible—but still at a window."

But the two haven't driven off yet. First the woman sits down next to him on the pedestal in the Saragossa bus station and says, "Well?" He has the feeling he's seeing her from the front for the first time. She's beautiful. And that's something very rare, and not only for the transitional time when this story takes place. And as she then listens to him, as he takes a bite from the bitterest of his bitter steppe mushrooms, and lets the bitterness spread from the middle of his tongue to the tips of his hair and his toes, then finally forces his lips apart and for the first time— since when?—makes his voice heard, she seems to be taking the words right out of his mouth. He breaks out in a sweat, different from the cold sweat of a while earlier. She laughs. Is she laughing at him? His heart begins to bleed. So there is such a thing? There is. So finally his heart is bleeding, and he can speak again, first only in a cry: "What do you want of me? What do you want of me, dear one? Tell me what you want of me!"

Along with his recovered ability to speak, or in the moment before that, love shot into him, accompanied by the thought: "Too late. Much too late, much too late!" And then he said approximately the following: "Crap. Him again. Her again. Well, well. So what. Crap. Not long now. When was that? Someone was fond of me once. Not just one person. And not just once. Crap. And I? Fond only for the moment. Then out of sight, out of mind. Was fond and then alone again. Unavailable. Crap. Life for! Life for whom? The noble types. Oh, the many noble types! Who will save them? Who will protect their rights? Something that awakens them from the dead! A monument to the peddler on the steppe. Crap. How happy I once was that I had children. Consecrated by them. My wife also my child. My mother also my child. Father, my dear child! Grandfather, strange little boy. Crap. Everything will be all right again. Everything was never all right. Today it's actually better than ever before. Why does the feast of the Ascension come before the celebration of the birth? 'I don't recall': That was the standard response of my father's mother. Or of my mother's mother? 'I don't recall.' And the way she said that, it remained one of the most wonderful sentences I've ever heard. 'I don't recall.' All her sons but one lost in the war. She died quietly of cancer. Oh, crap! And that I was just standing on the stone bridge over the Ebro—that was also long ago. And if I don't get home soon now, I won't ever get home."

And then the two of them fall into each other's arms. Or she catches him. And since he's heavy, there's a hollow thud. But even then they don't set out yet. First they have coffee in the bar at the bus station, not coffee from the blue mountain on Jamaica, and in a glass instead of a cup. In the restaurant there the winner removes a feather from his hair—not one from an eagle of the steppe—clips his fingernails—no one is watching—switches the shoes that he'd put on the wrong feet—how could he walk so far with them that way?—and gives him an outfit that he changes into in the men's room.

Is this suit one of her deceased husband's? She says nothing; altogether hardly speaks; speaks only once, already in the bus, in the moment before they start up: "In your medieval epics there are cases in which a man who loves a woman wrong, and wrongfully takes her as his wife, receives a magic potion that gives him the illusion of possessing her at night, and that for his whole life. Nowadays, however, this impression occurs and persists without a magic potion—a long-standing and widespread phenomenon. The man I was with merely imagined he was with me. And how insulting even that illusion was! Therefore, as soon as he was dead, I had his things removed from my house. And before his death I made sure he understood that everything between him and me was all a chimera. And long before my husband's death it was decided! If I should ever be inflamed with love for someone again, the first thing I would do is beat him up, at first sight!"

The driver didn't take my storyteller home by the most direct route. Where they turned off each time, he didn't tell me, and I didn't want to know, either.

What did the two of them experience together? He told me only about what they heard and saw. Even shared smelling or sniffing was out of the question for his way of storytelling. "Outside Pamplona we saw the first snow on the Pyrenees. In Biarritz we listened to the sea by the lighthouse bluff; it was so wild there, with a surf that seemed to be pounding from all sides, that we thought we were way out in the ocean on a tiny atoll. When we were sitting in a village near Toulouse, between the Garonne and the Canal du Midi, a child came and brought us things all afternoon—apples, stones, feathers, broken cassette tapes, rubber bands, two wine grapes, two little fishes, a dead mole, and finally a drawing that purported to be of us. In the salt works near Narbonne we climbed up the ridge of the salt-bearing mountain, sat on top and stared into the empty, rocky countryside, while beneath us salt crystals crunched, louder and louder. A day's journey farther to the north we heard, somewhere in a deciduous forest, a screeching like the brakes of cross-country bikes, high above our heads, and saw the limb of a tree lying in the fork of the tree next to it, and as the wind rubbed the two limbs together and rocked them, it made a screeching and a whining and now and then also a sighing. One day and one night later we spent hours watching two cats courting. And having left a few more river, mountain, and climate divides and borders behind us, we stopped on the almost abandoned pass through the Alps and looked out the curved windows of the bus, which magnified the view, out over a snow-covered, smooth white mountain landscape, stretching in undulating rises, without rock outcroppings and cliffs, under the bluest sky and the warmest, quietest sun, and, in the few places where it formed hollows and curves, signs of the courses and meanders of small brooks under the deep snow—an additional shimmer of sun, a 'blaze,' they used to call it, and, where two trickles probably converged in the depths of the eternal snow, in a broad dip that was traced especially gently by the snow amidst the pure white hummocks, one small area in shadow, to which, however, the blaze also penetrated, shimmering more warmly than anywhere else, hot. And we didn't drive constantly or just stop, but also walked now and then together over hill and dale, and I think anyone who'd seen us that way, even one who'd long since stopped dreaming about men and women, would have felt his heart beat higher at the sight of the two of us going along—at least for a moment, at least from afar!"

And on such a walk she spoke another of her sentences during the trip home: "That's why you attracted me so, for better or for worse, because I once heard it said of you that you were the only man between the Untersberg and the Straits of Penedes who seemed as though he had a story to tell, even though it was a far sadder one than that of Aeneas and his flight from the burning Troy." And during another such walk together she said to him, "I lay in the wooden shack on the edge of the steppe as long as was necessary for me to become pure again."

Was there such a thing? Could one regain one's purity? And what then?

One fall evening they reached the environs of Salzburg. The woman parked the bus at the airport, and they walked together in a westerly direction on a road through the fields, toward his house. They saw every image razor-sharp, heard every sound as if for the last time. And suddenly he dreaded the remainder of his life, or the days that were to come, or initially just the next day without her, and he said, "Stay with me." And she said, "No. Don't you know it's too late, at least for the two of us—perhaps not for other couples." And he said, "But you asked me for help." And she said, "You've already helped me." She turned and went back to her bus, and he continued on his way home. But in their good-byes, it was as if both of them were bursting into bloom.

In the only shop, already closed, on his street along the border-river dike, the display window was lit up—what, were Advent calendars being sold already? On the other hand, in Saragossa, too, the lottery ticket vendors had already been hawking the Christmas lottery on street corners, in the middle of October.

Large autumn leaves had blown far into the shop. And he climbed onto the dike behind it for a look at the Saalach, the border river. What was the river doing? It was flowing. And having arrived in front of his house, he noticed that without realizing it he was already holding the key in his hand—since when?—clutching it.

The house was dark. He didn't go inside yet, despite the stormy weather, with wind and rain. A neighbor's child came along the otherwise deserted street and said in passing, "I know you. You live here. This is your house. You're the pharmacist of Taxham." That's how caringly the child spoke. And his car was standing in front of the house, its engine crackling, as if it were just cooling down.

First, a turn through the garden. All the fruit harvested, except for a few figs on the tree, one of them popped into his mouth as he passed. So was there such a thing, fig trees, and with figs that ripened, this far north? Yes, in the meantime almost everything could be found everywhere.

He moved about with eyes closed, as if someone were leading him by the hand. Eyes open! Beneath the cedar, which had meanwhile wandered from his neighbor's yard into his own, there was a glow in the dark from three and nine and fifteen, from twenty-seven parasol mushrooms, no, even twenty-eight knee-high ones, from all of which the rain was dripping as it does only from parasol mushrooms. "As for you, we're going to leave you here for now!" (He said "we.")

In front of the door, stumbling over something unfamiliar: a tree root had broken through the earth there, and now its entire length protruded unevenly in front of the entry. When he opened the door upstairs to his wife's part of the house, there was a racket as if from an object falling to the floor, a rather small and light object. To judge by that, his wife had probably gone out as usual, but was back from her holidays and again living in her area, separated from his: Even invisible, her things gave evidence of that, in their always highly unstable order, with only a breath of air somewhere needed to bring things tumbling and crashing down.

"Of course it wasn't the mushrooms that drove us apart," said the pharmacist of Taxham. "One time—I don't know when or how—I must have hurt this woman so badly that without really being irreconcilable she couldn't stand to be with me any longer. But she couldn't leave the house, either. And it seems to me that the two of us aren't the only people like that."

In his part of the house, everything was as he'd left it. The only mail a couple of postcards from his daughter on her holiday island, from which she'd meanwhile long since returned to the pharmacy that would one day be hers. "Dear

Father," two words that did him good. And then the pathologist's report on the small growth on his forehead that had been removed back in the summer. "And?" He didn't tell me.

He sat down in the dark facing the blank white wall, where, in the light of the river-street lamps, the shadows of the garden trees tossed in the storm, thrusting forward like animals and snapping back, then during quiet moments like runners in the starting blocks—and now a lightning start! He closed his eyes, and behind his lids saw the delicately sparkling soil of the steppe, stretching far, to the ends of the earth. Gradually the house became populated with his dead. Was his son among them again? "No, not this time."

An ax struck him in the neck, and his head landed with a thump on his chest. The execution? No, he'd merely fallen asleep. But his head had fallen forward with such force that he could have broken his neck, just sitting there quietly. How dizzy he was. Into bed. No, no sleeping yet.

Down into the cellar, a place in the house that he'd always avoided before. But today he felt at home in this underground spot, as if arrived. And it wasn't filled with those foreign interlopers he'd dreamed about one time, but empty and silent.

Upstairs again to read. Reading light on. A glance at his shoelaces, because of something eye-catching: a faded thing entangled in one of them and sticking out—a stalk of steppe grass. Opening the epic of *Ivain, or the Knight with the Lion.* Where had he stopped reading? So he'd set out so abruptly that he'd forgotten to put in a bookmark?

At last he found his place. He read on. But suddenly he paused and began to tremble. Now he was trembling. Only now was he trembling.

I had a meeting with the pharmacist in the middle of winter, during night duty in his Taxham pharmacy, that curious flat bunker on the open expanse of grass right in the center of the village, surrounded by scattered apartment houses.

And he spent more than half the night telling me his summer story, with a few interruptions. Once an old woman came in and picked up a chest-pain powder that allegedly only he knew how to make. The second time the bell rang it was already past midnight; a young father was bringing his child, who had fallen out of bed and hit his head, which was bleeding and was now dabbed and bandaged by the pharmacist in his white lab coat. It was also already very late when a cry for help was heard from nearby, and the pharmacist immediately leaped to his feet—even if the cry came from a late-night movie on television. Another time a loud howl suddenly went up outside, animal-like, as if a dog had been run over, and the sound was magnified inside the laboratory: a man of indistinct age who seemed assailed by unbearable pain, or perhaps more by sorrow and misery, but without being able to communicate except by means of such howling, combined with a few gurgled, completely incomprehensible syllables; this went on for a while, accompanied by wringing of hands, his eyes wide open, as he unleashed his anguish on the pharmacist, face to face, and then just as suddenly fell silent and vanished into the darkness.

Remarkable how no matter what he was doing, whether mixing a powder or tending to a wound, the pharmacist worked in the smallest space, with hardly an expansive gesture, and also remained almost soundless; so his style of working had changed? And of his medications he handed out only the smallest units, the smallest boxes, or only single pieces; the powders and elixirs by the spoonful; and he had spoons lined up in water glasses, like Balkan hospitality spoons—except that instead of being intended for honey, they were for medicines.

Watching him warmed me. Even though he remained solitary in his work, it could be felt that he was doing it for someone, for others. And these absent others were all his kin.

But one time someone came out of the night whom the pharmacist ran to meet while he was still at a distance, then twisting the man's arm behind his back, even though he was waving something like a proper prescription, and pushing him away, wordlessly, almost violently.

At some point, long before the wintry dawn, the pharmacist was done with his story and brewed us his coffee from the Blue Mountains, just the smell of which did something to me.

Then we stepped outside, onto the grassy patch with a few rose bushes, one of which still had a blossom at the very top; and in the earth beneath it there were still a couple of strawberries, pale red, but edible. The pharmacist had exchanged his lab jacket for a coat, but even without that it seemed to me as if at the first step the medicine smell had dissipated.

I observed him from the side. I don't know why I've always had this reluctance to describe people—their faces, their bodies, especially particular features—and why I read such descriptions, no matter how skillfully done, with distaste, as if they were unseemly. Nevertheless, this is perhaps the moment at least to suggest the pharmacist's appearance: He wasn't especially large, but instead broad, with broad shoulders, and the most noticeably broad part of him, in fact the only noticeable thing about him, was his nose: with permanently distended nostrils. A little unusual also was his rather dark—not tanned—skin; in this connection he told me, another time, that during his student days he'd been involved in theater and had appeared in a free adaptation of the Mesopotamian Gilgamesh epic—as the king? He ignored my question.

And then it occurred to me how in my childhood so many people on the street had seemed to me copies of the movie stars of the time, and how in the meantime that never happens to me anymore—except now with the pharmacist of Taxham, who reminded me of Gary Cooper, Pedro Armendariz, and other heroes, and at the same time of comics like Stan Laurel, Jerry Lewis, and especially Buster Keaton; but also of female stars, those apparently unapproachable ones; and even of screen villains like Edward G. Robinson and Ernest Borgnine. That didn't result from any similarity, but perhaps from the story I'd just heard, but certainly even more from his way of looking and following things that happened: In his eyes, everything seemed to have the same tempo; there was no difference between speed and slowness; a car passing at top speed was met with the same quiet gaze from him as the steam rising from his glass coffee cup. But hadn't he told me something altogether different? That speed could fill him with panic, even just as an observer?

And I asked him whether he'd been changed by his story.

He replied, "In the middle of it, I swore to myself once that if I ever came back here, it would be as a changed person! But the only thing about me that seems to have changed is that my feet are bigger; I had to buy new shoes."

And I asked him why he'd become a pharmacist.

"That was because of my clan," he replied, "a pharmacist clan. Back in the High Tatra we even had our own coat of arms."

And then he asked me in turn whether I'd intentionally not taken notes. I affirmed that.

"That's fine," he said, "the main thing is that you write a sweeping account of what I've just told you. Otherwise it'll all have been for naught. But I want to have it in black and white. I want to have my story in writing. From speaking it, orally, nothing comes back to me. In written form, that would be different. And in the end I want to get something out of my story, too. Long live the difference between speech and writing. It's what life's all about. I want to see my story written. I see it written. And the story itself wants that."

"But who else is supposed to get to read the story?" I asked. "After all, what kind of storytelling do we have nowadays— not in the marketplace, not at the royal court, not for a middle class, not even addressed to an individual—merely for the person to whom the story happened, himself?"

He responded, "Perhaps precisely this is the original form of storytelling? This is how it first began?"

No stars. The sky over Taxham completely black, except for a brief moment of moonlight from behind a cloud shaped like a Venus shell. "Tarsenefyde!" the man next to me exclaimed.

The nocturnal wind was blowing here, too, hardly noticeable but just as potent. It was as if a second wind were blowing along with it, one intended specially for us standing there outside, a mere caress. And we let it make the hair on our necks stand on end. And behind us now the chirping of a cricket. In the middle of winter? Yes. And the chirping came not from below but from above, from a crack in the pharmacy wall. And farther off in the darkness a drunk was staggering along.

"No," the pharmacist said, "I know him. He's not drunk; his wife and children have left him. I'll at least say hello to him." And he went over and did so. And elsewhere in the darkness a very young girl went by, in her arms an infant that seemed to have just been born.

The pharmacist took a few more steps into the night. Steppe steps? More like those of a small child, legs splayed to avoid falling. And in the direction in which he now pointed, his face twisted over his shoulder toward me, the current wars were being fought, since the transitional time when his story takes place. And suddenly, with the stone he unexpectedly hurled into the blackness, it seemed as if he could easily join the fighting, as violent as anyone else. So in that respect, too, he'd changed? And already he was back in the pharmacy, and already outside again, with a burning newspaper, which he tossed after the stone.

"In retrospect I realized," he said later, as we were sitting, toward the end of the night, at the small table in his laboratory, "that I'd always been half-consciously expecting that blow, out there on the edge of the airport forest—but in the stomach instead of on my head. By the way, when you get to the place where I strike my son, I'd advise you to write that I merely raised my arm to strike him—not to soften it, on the contrary: To raise your hand, especially against your own child, without striking is more despicable, or at least uglier and more disgusting, than actually striking him."

And after that I could finally put my questions to him better. I asked whether he was longing to experience another adventure like this year's. "A strange year!" was all he said. And then: "Here I'm often happy, with myself and my work. But then that isn't enough for me. That's how loneliness sets in, and with loneliness comes guilt."

"Guilt because of one mistake or another, and omissions in the course of your story?"

"Yes, I did a few things wrong in my story. And when the time comes, I'd like to do something wrong like that again. Whatever I'm doing here, I'm ready for the next adventure— the next significant distraction. And it's perhaps less longing than greed. Just as my master Paracelsus said, in his fragment on mushrooms: He who catches sight of something precious is, in the same moment, already on the lookout for the next precious thing. Except that I can't seem to find that particular black-glowing entrance again. At the time of my story, I had it. What wouldn't I give to find that entrance once more!"

"The clearing in the airport forest, with the sycamore and the spring—is it still there?"

"It's been bulldozed and drained, for new housing. And that's all right."

"And your two traveling companions, the poet and the Olympic medalist—do you still meet them here occasionally?"

"Yes, in the root-cellar restaurant. Besides, why should I avoid the restaurant and the two of them? They're chance acquaintances, and to this day they've shown no surprise that I can speak now, when back then I was mute. I often feel a more lasting bond with chance acquaintances than with friends, and it's less dangerous."

"And the nocturnal-wind town?"

"The majority in the streets there has seized power, and is on the way to having its own state. One of the current wars is taking place there, and its main theater is the open steppe."

. . .

And from then on my questions were limited almost entirely to "And?" — "And?" — The pharmacist: "One day she'll come into my house, the woman who's not my enemy." — "And?" — "Don't you feel this, too? It's as if there were no one left of my own age: People either all seem much older than me or much younger." — "And?" — "Yet I feel a growing-old in myself, in that my energy, which continues to be there, perhaps stronger than ever, is no longer accompanied by any drive to actualize it. Something lies before me, seemingly expecting me to get it going, and I walk right by it." — "And?" — "A person usually remembers how a dream ended. Almost never how it began!"

And then I questioned him more searchingly after all: "Can you sing?"—whereupon he, who had been speaking all night with considerable effort, always on the verge of becoming voiceless, of merely moving his lips (just watching him was painful), stood up, bent over the sheaf of steppe plants—actually as thick as a sheaf—inhaled as deeply as possible, then letting his breath out, launched into a singsong, and was suddenly really singing, in a voice less powerful than penetrating, the following song, which sounded as though it had been in preparation a long time and practiced in private:

They fell into each other's arms with unspeakable weakness.
They had unspeakable joy of one another.
They lay together in unspeakable exhaustion.

They awoke in unspeakable amazement.
They looked out all the windows with unspeakable
   impatience.
They drove on with unspeakable patience.

They loved one another unspeakably.
They grew unspeakably free with one another.
They grew unspeakably bold with one another.
They grew unspeakably grateful with one another.
They rewarded one another unspeakably.

They perspired,
   shouted,
   wept,
   bled,
   fell silent and
   told each other unspeakable stories.

They parted in unspeakable sadness.
They went in different directions
   in unspeakable anger
   at the unspeakable.

No one else in distress came to the pharmacy that night. "What do you need?" were always the pharmacist's first words. And for hours we sat there in silence, waiting for the predicted snow.

A dark, clear December day dawned, in the center of the Taxham triangle, between the runways, the rail line, the highway, all distinctly audible and distinguishable. The pharmacist saw me to the door, and I recalled the time when in the morning I hadn't wanted to get down to writing until the first flights of birds across the sky. We stood there a while.

Then I said, "I'm reluctant to write about the steppe in your story. First of all: where does such a steppe still exist in Europe? And then I don't like the word. 'Steppe.' It seems overused."

The pharmacist's reply: "But my story doesn't take place on a 'meadow,' and also not on a 'prairie.' It was the 'steppe'! I went onto the 'steppe.' I crossed the 'steppe.' There are certain words for which no substitutes exist, words that even keep the same form over thousands of years, very few—for instance *rossignol*, the nightingale, which was written in the medieval epics exactly the way it is today, or *la joie*, joy, or *la gué*, a ford, or *le droit*, right, or *perdu*, lost. And there's also the steppe, the region. Almost all Spanish towns are located by themselves on the steppe, hundreds of steppe miles from the next town, Ávila, Salamanca, even Madrid. The Alhambra in Granada is located on a rocky promontory overlooking the steppe. From the Mezquita in Córdoba it's a few steps to the Río Guadalquivír, and from there onto the steppe, where the goats drag their full udders along. Even here in Taxham there's the steppe, or, as it's rather pejoratively called, steppification, and not only on the railroad embankment and the place that's kept free for the circus, which in any case doesn't come anymore. And in my lab, that's a steppe bouquet, not flowers, just their empty, indestructible, endlessly varied calyxes and holders. Never will I throw away this bouquet! One time I sat on the steppe by a lone tree and received a nudge from behind, as if from a horse, urging me to ride on: This nudge came from the steppe tree's trunk in the wind. It was and is the steppe, and it has to be called 'the steppe.' And you have to make the reader eager to experience the steppe—and also afraid of it, within reason. Smell this! I'm not really sure whether the sense of smell has the strongest memory. But when exercised regularly, it certainly prevents forgetfulness. And here, taste this: a dried bitter steppe mushroom, good for headaches, sensations of unreality or madness, all forms of blarney, muteness, the staleness of being alone."

"This is the prescription man speaking," I thought—and only now saw the scars on the pharmacist's forehead, and that they weren't completely healed yet.

And he said, after a pause, "Out there on the steppe, now and then I was even thrilled with myself, amazing for an older person, and particularly amazing for me. And believe me, or look: No one can be trusted who isn't thrilled with himself at least now and then."

Long before the first bird, a jogger turning up—so there were joggers in Taxham now?—coughing and gasping, as if he were calling for his mother in the middle of the last world war.

And, after another pause, the pharmacist: "And besides, you have to slip into my story the word 'pause.' 'He paused.' First of all, it's an expression that sounds poetic in German— *innehalten*—and then pausing gives strength, is an intervention, in the course of events, in the blind course of events, in the world's blind course of events, in the flood of phenomena, in all the talk, including your own inner flood, and good for racing of the heart, rushing in the ears, stomachache, and many other things."

And after a longish such "pause," a final prescription: "Write nothing but love stories from now on! Love and adventure stories, nothing else! — Someone went away. The house became silent. But something was still missing: I hadn't heard a certain door close."

"Come on now, snow!" one of us said. And in fact a flake now flashed. "Here it comes, the snow!" we said in unison.

And now the first bird appeared on this morning, a fat raven, who screeched and squawked and craned his neck as if he were choking down a snake.

"Go ahead, raven, screech and squawk," said the pharmacist of Taxham in the voice that had almost been failing him for a long time now, the voice that first had to find its way out of him: "I know perfectly well you can also do otherwise."

Summer/Fall 1996